Dear Heather,

Bloooood!!.!

Jil.

,50

BLOOD MERCY
THICKER THAN WATER

STORY BY
JULIA BUSKO & JANEEN IPPOLITO

WRITTEN BY
JANEEN IPPOLITO

ILLUSTRATED BY
JULIA BUSKO

Uncommon Universes Press LLC

373 Allegheny Street

Meadville, PA 16335

www.uncommonuniverses.com

This is a work of fiction. Names, characters, businesses, places, events and incidents are either the products of the author's imagination or used in a fictitious manner. Any resemblance to actual persons, living or dead, or actual events is purely coincidental.

Edited by Sarah Delena White

Cover Design/Interior Illustrations by Julia Busko – www.juliabusko.com

ISBN-10: 0-9974099-5-9

ISBN-13: 978-0-9974099-5-6

To my husband,
who always believes in my imagination and never lets me give up
-Janeen Ippolito

For Mom and Dad,
who always encouraged me to work hard towards a goal
-Julia Busko

CONTENTS

Shortly after the fall of the Roman Empire, Melrose Durante formed the Houses of the Dead to help the Blood Kind, those humans afflicted with the blood curse. Forming a nongovernmental force gave the Blood Kind political rights within other countries and people-groups and created a community to oppose vampirism and the dark magic associated with it.

As a renowned intellect and healer, Melrose brokered deals among different organizations to enable Blood Kind to access blood transfusions as a way to stave off the appeal of vampirism. The first House formed was his own, Cryptaro, named because they used to seek refuge in catacombs and crypts. Melrose chose the term "Houses of the Dead" because Blood Kind were often sent to such houses. It is also a reminder to Blood Kind of how fragile their immortality truly is.

Cryptaro House - of Wisdom
Head: Melrose Durante
Strain Side Effect: obsessive compulsive disorders, mental processing disorders, schizotypal disorders
Abilites: a variety of savant skills or increased intellect in select areas. Cryptaro Blood Kind prefer quiet, routine lives in highly-controlled environments. Some still live in crypts.

Vectorix House - of Protection
Head: Vir Vectorix
Strain Side Effect: sensory processing disorders
Abilities: enhanced senses and strength. Vectorix Blood Kind police the other Houses and can ally with local law enforcement if the government approves.

Talamar House - of Commerce

Head: Gabrel Talamar

Strain Side Effect: narcissism, histrionics, bi-polar disorder, psychopathy

Abilities: mesmerism and highly developed social awareness. Talamar
Blood Kind often excel in business, politics, and the arts.

Paxena House - of Separation

Head: ruled by a rotating council

Strain Side Effects/Abilities: all strains welcome as long as they are
willing to abide by the Rules of Separation and serve other members of
Paxena House. Paxena House members believe the blood curse makes
them unsuited for interaction with healthy humans and that living in
isolated colonies is the best solution.

Lucasta House - of Neutrality

Head: Natalie Fiori

Strain Side Effect/Abilities: none. Only healthy humans may join Lucasta
House. It is formed by various clans of vampire slayers who have a truce
and/or partnership with the Blood Kind. However, Lucasta House still
views the Blood Kind as a ticking bomb.

Regeleus House - of Mercy

Head: Akira Yamamoto

Strain Side Effect/Abilities: all strains welcome. Healthy humans are also
welcome. Akira Yamamoto formed Regeleus House as a collective of rehabilitation houses for vampires who want to return to the Blood Kind fold.
The House also includes shelters for normal humans who have Blood Kind
ancestry and are coping with minor side effects or domestic issues.

PROLOGUE
A Vampire's Confession

Girard awoke in darkness. For a moment, the pitch black consumed his thoughts, leaving only the sound of his heart beating like a moth trapped in a jar.

Breathe in, breathe out. Panic wouldn't help him escape.

His fingers slid on the ground around him. Pockmarked cement beneath his fingers and behind him a rough metal wall. Some sort of cell? A cold, wispy echo of air above him proved there was enough room to sit up, so he did, his legs trembling. Beads of sweat trickled down his back beneath his traditional vestments of black trousers, black shirt, and round white collar.

"There's a chair behind you, priest."

The man jumped, his arms flailing out. One of them connected with a hard surface. Pain shot through his palm. More careful inspection revealed a metal folding chair with a cushion on the seat. He eased himself up into the chair. If he was going to die soon, he might as well be comfortable.

"Better, yeah?" The voice was feminine, with a trace of a gravelly drawl. "I wish I could say this would be a short visit, but that'd be lying. But I get that you have a whole flock to oversee, so I promise it won't be more than a few hours."

The priest gulped. "A few hours? What do you—what do you mean? What am I doing here?"

A soft chuckle from across the expanse. Or from right in front of him. It was too dark to tell. "Think back, Father. What's the last moment you remember?"

"I don't see what that has to do with-"

"Just. Think." A sigh. "Please."

Something in the plaintive undertone pushed his mind into action. "I had just received a call. A shut-in, new to our congregation, wanted to make a confession and couldn't come to the sanctuary. I was on my way to meet her…"

"And so you have." Now he could feel the woman in front of him, her warm breath blowing across his face in another, heavier sigh. "I'm Lucy. Forgive me, Father, for I have sinned. It has been five years since my last confession."

He blinked, but his mouth automatically formed an answer as his hands made the sign of the cross. "Go on, my child."

"I've killed fifty. Seventeen men, twenty women, and three children." Her voice caught. "The children were the hardest."

"Wait!" The woman's words sank into his mind, then rose to the surface once more, swirling in eddies of confusion. "What you're saying is impossible. You're a murderer—and to kill that many people—why confess—?"

A pause. "It's complicated."

While part of the priest recoiled in shock, another part numbly did the math. Leftover accountant skills from the time before his call to ministry. "Seventeen men, twenty—twenty women, three children—that doesn't add up to fifty people."

"They weren't all people."

"What were the other ten?" He braced his arms against the sides of the chair, not quite wanting to hear the answer.

"Vampires." Eerily calm. Matter-of-fact. "Human, but badly twisted. Separated from everyday life."

His heart froze for a moment. Then a laugh burst from his throat. "You can't be serious. Vampires are creatures from mythology and fiction. Urban legends. Metaphors for the decay of life and the isolation of sin."

"Yes, you did preach a homily on that a few Sundays ago. It was one of the reasons I chose you. You weren't afraid."

"Afraid of what?"

"To speak about the unspeakable and treat it seriously. To engage the monsters around mankind, even in normal humans. I appreciate that." There was warm breath on his face once more. He feared that if he reached out, he might touch the mad woman. "I can speak about it too, but for me it isn't a leap of faith."

"Why not?"

"Because I'm a monster. I'm a vampire." She inhaled. The tip of her shoe tapped on the floor. "And I'm about to do something very bad. Even for me."

CHAPTER ONE
ICE CREAM HEADACHE

"She looks sad."

Zeke's left hand squeezed Melrose's tightly. His other hand clung to the ice cream cone, almost crushing the waffle crisp. For a six-year-old, the child had an astonishing grip. If Melrose didn't know better, he would think his goddaughter's son had supernatural strength.

It would seem ridiculous for a child to posses supernatural strength. But given the child's heritage, it wouldn't hurt to give Zeke another medical examination before Melrose departed in a few days.

Currently, the child needed a napkin or twenty and a thorough hand-washing. At least they were at a public park. Someone else could be responsible for cleaning up the mint chocolate chip mess dripping onto the ground.

"Uncle Mel?"

"Yes, curious one?"

Zeke's eyes, round and dark, stared up at him through black bangs. His mouth puckered in frustration, wreathed with cream.

"We need to talk to her! See why she's sad."

"Who?"

"The lady over there!" Zeke's iron fingers loosened. His left hand swung out, index finger pointing a few benches away.

"Where?"

Melrose followed his charge's index finger across the park. A patchwork of green grass, cut through with cobblestone sidewalks. Pockets of trees stood along the paths, obstructing the view beyond a few meters and shading the ground with their thick layers of leaves. Ideal for a day as hot as this one.

Sweat clung to his skin beneath the protective layers of button down and blazer. But it was safer. No danger of melted ice cream on his skin. Clothes could be washed in quality detergent, but skin required careful inspection.

He continued scanning the park. There was no woman.

"Ezekiel, I'm afraid you are mistaken." Melrose kept his tone gentle, but firm, staring into the child's face. "Unless you see something I don't? Something your father sees?"

"No, but she was right-" Zeke's head swiveled back and forth. Then he exhaled in disappointment. "There. Nowhere. Sorry, Uncle."

"No matter." Melrose pushed his charge's hair back from his forehead. Cooler, but still warm. This little excursion needed to end. "Come, we must return to your parents."

"Okay."

Melrose stood, tugging Zeke along the path. He scuffed his small sneakers along the cobbles, his face flushed despite his t-shirt and shorts. Compassion stirred within Melrose. The child was too well-behaved to ask, but that didn't mean he didn't require a rest.

"Ride on my back?"

A grin dimpled his round face. "Yeah!"

"Very well." Zeke's weight would make it twice as hot. Melrose only knelt on the ground, his knees balanced on the uneven stones. "Climb up. But no ice cream."

Zeke nodded and threw the remainder into a nearby trash bin. Smeared his hands on his shorts. "Up, up, in the-"

His words disappeared in a muffled yelp. A blunt force struck Melrose's neck, vibrating through his shoulders and spine. Another force smashed into his lower back. The ground rushed to meet him. He flung out his palms, catching himself on the rough stones. Wincing against the sharp pain.

Move. He had to move. For Zeke. Melrose shoved up mental blocks. Rolled to his side and pushed up against the ground, rising to his feet.

"Zeke." The word was a whisper, sinking into the pit of his stomach.

* * *

Electric guitars squealed in Lucy's head. The same set of chords pounding out a rhythm over and over to the fast beat of her sneakers on the concrete. Running through the bricked streets of Old Quebec, past outdoor cafes and stone row houses converted into galleries and specialty shops. Pushing aside too many tourists with cameras and shopping bags. Her calves burned as she veered up a narrow passage between two buildings.

All the while, the guitars kept playing. Lucy hadn't owned a music device in years. Not since Jean-Claude had stolen her life.

She tried not to think about it too much.

The kid lay limp in her arms. Knocking him out had been essential. Not that she enjoyed it any more. But maybe, just maybe, it would be easier this way.

He had long eyelashes, like paint brush tips curled on his pale cheeks.

She blinked and licked the sharp edges of her incisors. The sliver of pain focused her mind on the task at hand. Cut through the repeating guitars and dulled them to a corner of her brain. A drink would do even better. But the plastic bottles in the pack that thudded against her back were drained.

Lucy swallowed and glanced down at the kid again. No details on him, as usual. Jean-Claude never sent details through Conan, his chief lieutenant. He just emailed Conan the bare minimum— location, type of abduction, appearance of target—and then Conan passed the info on to her. Usually with one of his disappointed looks.

Five years, and Conan still viewed her like leftover meatloaf, fuzzy with mold. Not that it mattered. In fact, his disgust made life easier. Attachment was stupid and painful.

The kid squirmed in her arms, his lips pursing together in a frown. Her heart thudded. No.

He had to stay asleep. She couldn't do this to a conscious child.

She'd never even drunk from a dead one. Just turned them over to Conan and gotten her share of blood from the general supplies

A special mission, Jean-Claude sent. Something only Lucy could do. If she completed it, she'd get a rest. A real rest.

"He's lying."

"You don't know that." Lucy whispered. She frowned, and slowed to let a tour group past. A few spared her curious looks. The guitars whined through the chords again, this time much louder. "He might be telling the truth."

"He took everything from you," the voice scoffed. Like hers, but fiercer, with a thicker drawl. Clear as the daylight that threatened to scorch her skin through the long-sleeved trench coat and broad-brimmed hat. "You think he's being truthful now? Idiot."

"I don't have time for this!" She exited the passage. More tourists glanced her way. Lucy's breath caught in her desert-dry throat. She forced her lips into a smile that hid her teeth. Brushed a hand over the kid's black hair. "He's had a long day. The sun and all."

She ducked down a side alley, past some half-finished public art. Shoot. Now they'd tell the cops. Time to finish this. Drain the child, make it messy. Leave it there for the guy to find. Melrose Durante. Whoever he was. Probably another vampire overlord like Jean-Claude.

"Maybe they're in a turf war. Are you going to slaughter a child over a turf war?" The voice stung with disdain. "You're better than this, Lucy. This isn't us."

"No. I'm me. You're nothing." Lucy coughed and stumbled against a wall. Her mouth ached with thirst. For the taste of fresh blood filling her mouth, calming the music and the voice in her head. Sending her to ecstatic heights far better than sanity.

Maybe she'd forget all of this, for at least a few hours. After that, it'd be time to kidnap another priest. If she could face them.

There. A stack of wooden crates jammed beside a small dumpster. A bar dumpster, surrounded by trash bags and broken glass. The stench of beer stung her nose, but there was no time to be fussy. Lucy picked her way through the debris and sat on the crates, bracing her feet on the asphalt. The wood creaked and shook. Not that strong after all.

"Lucy, don't! There's still a chance."

"You always say that. Where's the chance here, huh? Now who's lying?" She propped up the kid in her arms. Don't look at the face. Aim for the neck.

The guitars screeched. She'd known the rest of the song once. Now, it didn't matter.

All that mattered was a drink.

"Wait."

A new voice. Flat and level and male. Lucy's muscles seized, and she held the child closer. Had the cops gotten here this fast? Or maybe one of those nosy tourists?

Both could disappear if necessary. And it was always necessary. After a drink. A quick one. Jean-Claude wanted this messy. Get a few gulps in now, and then finish the rest later.

Lucy bent over the child's small, fragile neck.

"No! Wait. You don't have to do that."

Much closer now. Who was this guy? Shouldn't he be quivering in fear or running away in panic? She tilted her head up, just enough to see a man in a long coat like hers, no hat, and skin the color of a latte.

Lattes. Those had been good. Before the turning.

"Go away."

"No."

He took one step forward, then another. His brown eyes trained on her, jaw set, as if approaching a wild animal. Did he have a gun? Why wasn't he shooting?

"I mean it! I'll kill you too. Get out of here!"

"Release him." His tone never wavered.

"So you can kill me once he's in the clear?"

"No. So I can try to save you."

CHAPTER TWO
WHAT'S IN A NAME?

"Liar. You'll kill me."

The woman's voice shook. Her bloodshot green eyes glared at him. Remarkable focus for a vampire. Particularly one whose hunched shoulders, sallow face, and general irritation indicated she was badly depleted in nutrients.

Then again, she had never been an ordinary woman.

"No. I won't." Each syllable was slow and steady. A part of Melrose ached with concern for the child, and for this husk gripping tightly to life. But that part didn't matter right now. Losing control only guaranteed both of their deaths. He needed to get closer. A long-range taser blast didn't always work against vampires. Particularly hungry ones. Besides, addiction was a powerful pull, combined with whatever occult symbols were undoubtedly carved into her skin. "But others will, if you don't listen to me. Put the child down. Come with me."

She gulped. Coughed, dry and harsh. "I need a drink. You don't understand."

Melrose hazarded another step forward, his dress shoe

crunching on something he really didn't want to think about. Both soles would be bleached when he returned home. "I understand you're badly starved. Have you eaten anything in days? Months?"

The vampire woman shook her head, her hat flipping back and forth. Revealing strands of short brown hair, mixed with gray. He remembered when it was long and dyed pure black, with brilliant blue streaks. "Don't need food. Conan said that. I only need blood. Pills and IVs and blood."

"Conan is an imbecile. You're human as much as anyone else. You know this. Why would contracting a blood pathogen change that? Your body still requires sufficient nourishment for-"

"I'm not human. Not like you. Not anymore." Her clear, high voice deepened as she spoke, as if giving her last words. "And I'm hungry."

She licked her cracked lips and drew them back to reveal sharp incisors. Some of the better dental caps Melrose had seen. Which meant she was worth something to Jean-Claude. A lot more than the usual vampires.

Naturally. Jean-Claude had certainly taken extra care with her brainwashing. As he had with this entire plan.

She crouched over Zeke again. Melrose gripped the taser in his holster. He needed to jar her. Somehow. "What's your name?"

"What?"

Another step. Within range. She just needed a little more distraction.

"Your designation. What your mother called you at birth." Two rings glinted on the fourth finger of her left hand. One a plain, tarnished band, the other featuring a dull red stone. Faint hope flickered in his heart. She still wore them. Did she remember why? "The name your husband used at your wedding."

"Husband?" She straightened. Clarity flashed over her face, calming the twisted desire for a moment. "Jane. My parents call me Lucy, but he always called me Jane. Lucille Jane-"

He whipped out the taser and fired at her face. The electrodes grappled onto her skin. She jolted, releasing Zeke. Melrose dropped the gun and dove to catch the child, his knees scraping the asphalt. The pants would be burned later.

Zeke settled heavily into his arms, a whimper escaping him. Melrose cradled the child close, exhaling. Breathing. A necessary mechanism he forgot in difficult situations.

And just as vital for Blood Kind and vampires as it was for uninfected humans.

He shifted Zeke to his left arm and fumbled for his cell phone with his right hand. Pressed speed dial 1.

"Zurina? He's entirely unharmed."

"Praise God." His goddaughter sighed in relief.

"Yes, truly." Melrose surveyed Lucille Jane's prone form. "Continue following Zeke's tracking chip. And bring a car. You and Akira will have a new guest at the manor."

"Of course." Her voice filled with compassion. "Man or woman?"

"Female. Intensive care wing." He frowned. "Full security measures."

"Why?"

He couldn't keep the sadness from his voice. "She knows Conan."

*　*　*

Trapped.

Trapped.

Trapped.

The word echoed to the beating of her heart, loud and throbbing in her ears. Each heavy thud accentuated by violins, screeching through a concerto. Her mother's favorite. "Spring" from Vivaldi's *Four Seasons*.

At least the violins were tuned better than the electric guitars.

Lucy turned over on the soft, flat surface. Sheets. Blankets. A bed, and a very comfortable one. Far nicer than the old cot she slept on at Conan's lair, or the cheap motel beds when she was out on a mission.

She rubbed her hands along the bedclothes, trying to stir her memories.

Trapped.

Trapped.

The man had trapped her. Brought out Jane instead of Lucy. Made her unguarded, lost in the happiest day of her life. The day that was a lie. Jean-Claude said it was a lie.

Which meant the man was a lie. The man who looked like Thoth. Who was a lie. It was all a lie, and the liar caught her.

Trapped her.

Zapped her.

Lucy's eyes snapped open, muscles tense. She lay on a bed in a small room. Plain beige walls, softened by the glow of recessed lighting. The hospital bed was the only furniture. Nothing to add clutter.

Nothing to use as a weapon.

Next to the bed stood an IV cart with a bag of fluids and a bag of red liquid. Blood. Both fed into her via clear plastic tubes to the back of her left hand. Lucy traced the tubes, bile rising her throat. Blood through IV? Obscene.

Her mouth still ached for the precious substance. She gripped the tube beneath her fingers, pinching hard. Maybe if she could just yank it out, pull out the needle, get the liquid down her throat—

A knock sounded at the door. "May I come in?"

"Who are you?" Just another second, and the needle would be out.

The door swung open. Lucy yanked her hand back from the needle.

"Zurina, but you can call me Zuri. Everyone does. You're in my house. A welcome guest." A woman padded into the room, bearing a tray of food. She was built like an athlete, with curves and muscle in equal proportion, and clad in what looked like a renaissance fair outfit: white blouse, black corset, and a long skirt with lacings up each side. Her tanned, heart-shaped face wore a gentle expression, reflected in her hazel eyes.

"You can't attack her." Jane's voice was rough with insistence. "She's an innocent."

Lucy scoffed, "We attack innocents all the time. Like the kid!"

"*You* attack them. I don't!"

Zuri paused, tilting her head to the side. "Would you like some time to reconcile with yourself?"

"What?" Lucy's face heated. She'd been saying that out loud. Now they'd bring out the strait jacket for sure. All because Jane couldn't stop butting into her life.

The violins spiraled into a dirge.

"You seem agitated with yourself. I can bring this food back at a later time. Perhaps when Uncle Melrose comes to give you another examination."

Melrose. The word lit up Lucy's mind like an electric shock. A sensation she was very familiar with. Jean-Claude enjoyed shocking people, literally. Especially her. His perfect little weapon. "Melrose? I need to talk to him!"

Zuri stopped in the doorway. "He's resting at present. You've been here over a day, and he spent most of that time seeing to your care. I can alert him when he's available."

"Now!"

CHAPTER THREE
GUILT AND ST. BERNARDS

Scrub. Rinse. Repeat.

From the edge of one tile to the next. Each grout line scrutinized for maximum cleanliness. Rubbed once more with the rag. Then on to the next line. There would always be more he could do.

More to cleanse. More to rescue. More to heal.

"Uncle?" Zurina's voice. No time to heed it.

He needed to focus. Needed to work, to do something.

Before the monsters came and took the last precious thing he had. No, they'd taken her already and turned her into a monster. A rare, unexpected gift in his life, tormented because she knew him.

Melrose swallowed. The edge next to the tub was the hardest.

"Uncle Melrose." Her low, level tones were much closer now. Zuri knelt on the ground next to him, sweeping her red skirt to the side. Her strong fingers gripped his hand. "I think three times over means the bathroom is clean. Even by your standards."

Melrose looked up from the floor, meeting his goddaughter's sweet face. She'd worn that compassionate expression since birth. So like her mother.

Her words cut through the compulsion. For the moment. He sighed, dropping the sponge and tearing his gaze away from the endless grout lines. Rubbing a hand over his close-cropped hair. All the easier to ensure maximum sanitation, short of daily shaving. Melrose was just vain enough not to consider that option.

"How long have I been here?"

"Not long. Only an hour." She sighed, brushing an errant curl of brown hair into her bun, and leaned against the sink cabinet that faced opposite the bathtub. "You examined Zeke. He's safe and healthy. You did everything right. And you even managed to rescue that poor woman. Lord knows what horrible things Conan did to her."

"Jean-Claude as well." The name caught in Melrose's throat. Zuri squeezed his hand again. "Yes, but she's safe."

"For now." The words came out shorter than he meant. Zuri never deserved that.

She only smiled. "Over two thousand years, and you think you'll fail? This is what you do, Uncle. And the reason Akira founded Regeleus House. We're meant to be a safe haven for those with nowhere else to turn. We'll help you."

It wouldn't be enough. But Melrose couldn't explain why. Couldn't let her get any closer to the truth. Not until he had figured it out on his own. "And what of your own House? What of the Vectorix?"

"Regeleus House is mine as well. I support Akira."

"And lie to him?"

A sudden burst of wind swirled through the room, rustling

the shower curtain. Zuri scowled at him. "Provoking arguments is beneath you."

"Self-deception is beneath you. What of the Vectorix? They need you."

"Debatable." Another gust. She winced, and the breeze ceased. So she had some control. "A debate between Father and myself."

"After five decades? A long debate." Melrose stood slowly, his feet tingling from lack of use. "Vectorix House is honored as the protector of the Blood Kind, Zurina. That was why I founded it with your father. You were raised to lead it."

"Yes, by you, not him. A long time ago." She stood as well, shaking the folds of her skirt. One hand lingering to smooth out the wrinkles, then reaching up to finger the embroidery on her corset. For a moment, she was nine years old, her hazel eyes large and plaintive as she asked if killing was the only thing Vectorix House did. "You and Father shouldn't be the only ones permitted to choose your own destinies."

Melrose frowned. "Sometimes destiny finds you as well. Don't be afraid of that."

"Now who sounds mystical? Are you the same stalwart scientist who taught me to question everything?" She smiled down at him. Utterly unfair that she inherited her father's height.

He shrugged. "I'm also the one who taught you to value other perspectives. I thought you would see when all logic points to a higher calling and duty to family."

"You're mentioning duty?" Curiosity flashed in her eyes.

"Is that a crime?"

Zuri shook her head, turning away towards the sink. Also white. Who made a bathroom entirely white? "No, only you've distanced yourself for five years. From a lot of duties."

Had his voice been that sharp? Melrose rubbed his hand across his forehead. "You're correct. That was necessary, but not fair. I apologize." He squeezed her shoulder. She answered with a faint smile. He continued, "At what point did two hundred years become 'long ago'?"

"When I became a mother."

On cue, the sound of thudding feet on hardwood floors echoed towards them. A moment later, Zeke's body slammed into her skirt, his cheeks red with exertion. "Mom! Uncle Melrose! Hide me!"

He scrambled behind them and hopped into the bathtub. The thudding continued, this time accompanied by loud scratches and growls and fierce barks. Melrose glared, clenching his hands into fists. Not now.

Not when everything was settling down. Safe.

He grabbed the door handle. Zuri's hand pressed against the panel, pushing back against his resistance. She shook her head with a sly glint in her eyes. "They're harmless."

"To you, perhaps."

"Facing your fears is helpful to growth. My uncle taught me that."

A moment later, two enormous St. Bernard dogs galumphed around the corner, their dark eyes filled with uncontrolled friendliness, their mouths leaking drool. At their broad heels ran two miniature dachshunds. Melrose barely ducked out of the way before they lunged at him.

He exhaled, watching as they mobbed Zuri and Zeke with a chorus of barks and joyful pawings. "Your uncle also apparently wasted his time cleaning the bathroom."

"I wasn't going to say anything. But this is one of Zeke's favorite places to hide." Zuri grinned, rubbing her hands on the St. Bernards' coats, heedless of the tricolored fur clinging to her clothes. On the floor, Zeke giggled helplessly as the smaller fiends licked his face.

The child was alive to do so. As was the woman who'd taken him.

In a manner of speaking, considering how Jean-Claude liked to experiment. Melrose sighed. "I suppose I should get changed, and check on the patient."

"Yes! Oh, I meant to tell you when you had stopped cleaning." Zuri pushed one dog away with a gentle shove on the nose. "Lucy demanded to see you. She said she had something to tell you."

His heart stopped. "She did?"

"Yes. She seemed to recognize your name."

* * *

Spiders slithered beneath her skin.

Lucy rubbed at her arms, itching from the sandpaper gown. What kind of messed up trick made cloth look like cotton, but feel like burlap? Not even Conan had subjected her to this. His torture had been direct, not hidden behind kind, smiling faces.

The violin changed from Vivaldi to a simple piece, one that repeated ceaselessly in her mind. Off-key, to make it worse.

"You learned it off-key." Jane's smug voice. "We've always played that piece off-key."

"Shut up." Lucy gripped the sheets. Her mouth begged for liquid, richer and darker and sweeter than water. "You're the reason we're here. You're weak. Frail. You let Melrose's lies, his eyes, capture us."

"His eyes hold the answers."

The door slid open. In walked the devil himself. Melrose Durante, in a pair of pressed khakis and a light blue button-down, the sleeves rolled up to the elbow. The clothes were tailored to his lean runner's form.

"His chest was plenty broad enough to sleep on. I wonder if he still shaves it."

"He's in the room!" Lucy hissed.

Jane shrugged their shoulders. "Now who's shy?"

An image flashed to mind. The man in front of them. Only instead of leaning against a wall, quietly observing Lucy, he was far closer, his stoic face studying her in open admiration, tracing her jaw with a fingertip.

"No!" She shoved the picture away. It didn't belong to her. Not anymore. Lucy was a vampire. Human relationships and desires meant nothing. She had a specific message to give. It should have been given while enjoying the blood of the child, but at least she could salvage part of her mission.

Perhaps, when she escaped, Conan wouldn't abuse her any more than normal. As long as Jean-Claude didn't visit, she could bear it.

"And you call me the weak one?" Jane's scornful tone pierced the air.

Lucy rolled her eyes. "This is *my* life."

"Is there a point the two of you will make eventually?" Melrose glanced at his watch, his full lips twitching. "Otherwise, I do have other duties."

Jane rose in Lucy's mind, stealing her voice. "More important than your own wife?"

Lucy bit her tongue, drawing a trickle of blood. The pain drew tears—despite it being less than a pinprick of Jean-Claude's preferred methods—but it blocked Jane from any further comments. Too much damage had already been done. As it was, Melrose studied her intently, his dark eyes softer.

"What do you mean?" He moved forward, stalking her with the same care he had in the alley. "Jane?"

Lucy sat up. Time to use that towards her advantage, and rip out the creep's heart while it still lay open in his perfect, latte-colored face.

"Jane is dead. Jean-Claude killed her. In five days, Quebec City will fall."

CHAPTER FOUR
IMPENDING DOOM AND OTHER NUISANCES

She was alive.

All Melrose knew was that simple fact. Jane lived. Mistreated and buried beneath this brainwashed veneer who called herself Lucy. But there nonetheless, and strong enough to push through the madness in brief, spicy bursts.

It was all Melrose could do not to shake the woman who sat on the hospital bed, her green eyes blazing with hatred. Rattle out the toxic persona that had taken hold of his Jane, and be rid of Jean-Claude's perverse influence forever.

If only it were that simple. God in heaven, he wished it were that simple.

Life never was.

Lucy's words registered, a wash of harsh vitriol likely meant to shake his resolve and wound him deeply. Especially the comment about Jane being dead, which would have been far more effective if she hadn't, in fact, emerged just a few moments prior.

Melrose raised his eyebrows. "The entire city, dead? That's ambitious for Jean-Claude. What nefarious scheme is he planning this time?"

"The streets of Quebec City will run red with blood to feed the rising tide of vampires. The Houses of the Dead will burn, and everyone you love, Melrose Durante, will perish in searing flames!"

"As opposed to non-searing flames?"

The woman blinked, her shoulders slumping. "Excuse me?"

"Presumably that entire speech was programmed into your mind, so please don't take this criticism personally. I mean it entirely towards your former overlord, who apparently still has a taste for melodrama." Melrose replayed her words in his mind. "Five days. Streets run red with blood. A quantity of vampires. The Houses of the Dead burned. Does that cover all relevant facts?"

"Every last one." Her wry tone lit his heart. "You'd think thousands of years would give Jean-Claude greater creativity."

"One would think." Melrose returned her impish smile despite himself. Snarky, sneaky Jane. The same woman who had caught his attention by taking illegal stock photos of him during a trip to Italy. Then, when he had demanded the footage, she'd only said he was taller up close.

He eased towards the bed. If he could only keep Jane talking, break through the persona. "I noticed you acquired some fascinating tattoos. And all this time, you insisted you never wanted any permanent marks."

His wife pushed up the sleeves of her hospital gown, tracing the symbols carved into her flesh. A haphazard array of circles and triangles, pierced with lines and dots. She grimaced. "Fun, right? They forced them on me. At least now you're not the only one."

"Yes, but mine were voluntary. In the days before." His were also actual occult symbols, now dead of their power and good riddance. Akira would have to verify, but Melrose wasn't sure the circles and triangles on Jane's flesh meant anything. Other than that her beautiful skin had been violated.

He stood beside her now. Close enough to touch her left hand. To trace the rings on her forefinger.

Jane flinched. His heart sank and he pulled away, but she placed her right hand over his. "Sorry. I never let anyone touch them, or take them off. I screamed and bit when they tried to make me. Jean-Claude laughed, but Conan got so mad at my disobedience that he took out his knife and carved and-" She shuddered, her eyes pinched shut. "-that only made Jean-Claude laugh more."

"He does that." Anger burned within him, but he quenched it with practiced ease. Melrose nudged onto the edge of the bed. Everything in him wanted to take her in his arms. Everything except the experience gleaned over the years, which reminded him of how fragile withdrawal was.

How easily things could take a turn for the worse.

* * *

Jane. Her name was Jane.

She clutched Melrose's hands between hers, focusing on the feel of his warm skin, his pulse. A pulse that kept time with the gentle strumming of an acoustic guitar. One of her favorite lullabies. A wandering musician had played it the night of their first date in Italy.

"I should have tipped him more," Jane muttered.

Melrose watched her, his face still tender, yet reserved. "Still hearing music in your head?"

She nodded. "I'd still take musical hallucinations over germaphobia any day. Did you have to burn the pants that touched the ground?"

"I considered it." He raised his eyebrows. As he always did when she brought up the side effects of the blood curse. The Cryptaro House had the strain that lead to neuroticism and compulsions. Occasionally hallucinations, such as with Jane. "But Zuri knows the proper methods of washing."

"And how to get you to calm down. Because she does everything perfectly." Bitterness edged her voice. Jane pulled her hands away from his. Felt Lucy surface with the anger. "She was always perfect, because you made her that way. You raised the perfect princess. What, am I not valuable enough? Is that why it took you five years to find me?"

Hurt flared in his eyes. Good. Melrose deserved to hurt. "I searched whenever I was able. I took time away from the Houses, from my own family-"

"I'm your family! Or has that changed as well? No, it was never the case. Otherwise you wouldn't have hidden me from them. That woman who came into the room, she had no idea who I was!"

A mask of control slipped over his face. The one he wore when facing enemies. "You don't even know who you are."

"You never told them! In five years!" Lucy's fingernails dug into her palms, drawing tiny trickles of blood. The guitar notes turned frantic. "Jane meant that little to you. That you never even admitted it to your family."

"That's not true. He was trying to protect us. Protect himself." Jane's voice, but barely a whisper.

Satisfaction filled Lucy. "Lies. He never loved you. You held on to nothing for five years. You have no husband."

Jane sighed. "No. He left."

Lucy glanced around the room. Nothing. She bared her teeth in a grin. "Good riddance. Good riddance to all of you! You'll all be dead in five days!"

She grabbed for the tube transfusing blood, and yanked.

CHAPTER FIVE
SYMBOLS AND STENCHES

"She's clean. No traces of takeover."

"Are you sure?" Melrose stared up at Akira, who stood across from him on the opposite side of Jane's bed.

He nodded, running his fingers through his thatch of black hair. His black eyes still fixed on Jane's unconscious form. More specifically, the area around her form, intently monitoring what only his brain could see. During Melrose's initial studies, Akira noted the demons stank of darkness and tasted of acrid, metallic smoke—then declined further explanation.

"*Oui.* She's being troubled, but it comes from her own soul, her own bitterness, not from demonic possession."

"Thank God." Melrose sighed, brushing a few strands of brownish-gray hair out of Jane's face. Premature graying. A reason she dyed her hair. The unnatural colors were merely a bonus. "Of course she is troubled."

"*Oui.* Not the only one." Akira rubbed his angular jaw. "Zurina, she watched the video feed. *Tres dévastée.* Tears coming down her face. Why you not tell her?"

Melrose mentally reordered the words. Akira Yamamoto had lived in English-speaking countries on and off for decades, and still hadn't mastered the language. He insisted that he had already learned the world's most perfect speech: French.

Entirely wrong. Latin and Italian were far superior. But English was the *lingua franca* at this point in time. How such an ugly, clumsy amalgamation of words came to reign supreme was beyond comprehension.

"It was too dangerous. I had planned to travel with Jane to meet all of you in person." Melrose drew his hand away. "Before I could, she had disappeared."

"*Je comprends.* You could not face it, the truth." His eyes gentled in sympathy. Zurina couldn't have chosen a man more different from her father. "She is here now. And you have our help."

Odd, to be comforted by a man barely a century old. Still, the depth of compassion in the Japanese man's eyes was genuine. He had experienced Jean-Claude's torture and experimentation first-hand.

"The symbols on her skin. Do you recognize them?"

Akira knelt and traced one of the markings on Jane's arms, frowning. He shook his head. "No. These aren't the occult signs I am familiar with." He shrugged deeper into his tan sweater. "Then, they spent more time up here with me."

He tapped at his head with a rueful look. Akira had started life as a healthy human with acute synesthesia, his senses cross-wired and interpreting the world far differently than normal. Jean-Claude had a special interest in pushing the boundaries of the extraordinary. Akira had suffered the results for years.

Even now, the strange gift of perception haunted Akira with visions into the spiritual realms. A gift he devoted to God—once he stumbled into a church in France and learned who God was. That the darkness he saw was real.

"Melrose? *Regardez ici.*" Akira held up one of Jane's hands. "The video showed her cutting her skin with her fingernails, *oui?* And taking out the needle?"

"*Oui.* Yes."

Akira gestured to Jane's unmarked palms. "Then why no scars?"

"That is a very good question." Melrose pushed up Jane's other sleeve and examined her arm. It had been a day since the incident. The high security room had a number of important features, including a mechanism to flood the room with fast-acting sedative vapors. However, the system to remove that sedative was far slower. Even now, faint amounts of the gas stung his nostrils.

A minor complaint. He stared at the carved symbols. The center of each was threaded with dark red blood scarring. Odd. Blood scarring usually healed within a month. Jean-Claude would have had to re-carve the symbols every two weeks.

An image of Jane strapped to a table as the vampire leader reopened all of those cuts. Painstakingly. With a smile on his face.

Melrose's chest burned with anger. Jean-Claude would pay. He could picture the man's face, his lips curved into a mocking smile. *Isn't that what you always promise, Thoth? And yet, here I am. Still haunting you.*

"Melrose?"

He looked up. Akira studied him with the same intentness that he fixed on Jane. Reading his distress. Melrose clamped down on the anger, and stood. "We're missing something. If these aren't occult symbols and Jane isn't possessed, then what was Jean-Claude doing with her?"

"His experiments always have some purpose."

According to Jane, they only had four days to discover it.

* * *

The house stank.

Regeleus Houses always did. Well, most of them. A smirk pulled at Conan's lips.

It reeked of devotion and prayer, the disgusting odor oozing from each window of the three-story Victorian and curling around the ornately carved railings. The stench reached Conan across the street, where he hid behind a tree growing through the sidewalk. More towered to his right and left in an orderly row, shading the smoothly-paved road and houses.

He tucked deeper into his coat, tipping the rain off his wide-brimmed hat. Luckily the day was rainy and overcast. It made going outside far more comfortable. The rain fell on the just and unjust.

But today, the just would fall. They had no idea. So easily deceived by their compulsive acts of kindness, taking in a woman off the street only for love. The fools. Conan killed any vampire in her condition on sight. Better to thin the herd for him and his ultimate vision.

Jean-Claude had other ideas. Always pushing the limits. Conan's smirk turned sour. The vampire leader had no sense of holding onto power. No, he had to play with it, play with people, try to gain more authority from his precious occult rituals. Never content with a solid stranglehold over the vampire populace.

Such playing produced the street mutt Yamamoto, who in turn blighted the vampires with his ability to see past the veil of the physical. A threat only due to Jean-Claude's inability to keep his hands out of people's skulls.

Conan spat, then glanced at the front porch again. Yes, there was the child, playing with his slobbering dogs. The brat should be dead. Lucy had failed at that too.

He had warned Jean-Claude she was rejecting vampiric

freedom. Her mind tainted by the putrid religion. She clung to the weakness of her hallucinations and her pathetic adoration for Melrose the Traitor.

Unlike Yamamoto, however, Lucy still had a great purpose. That purpose pleased Conan as much as it did Jean-Claude.

First, dealing with the child. A warning shot to the heart. Jean-Claude's personal message to the hypocrites. Especially Melrose.

He gripped the pistol in his coat pocket. Nothing equaled the nectar of fresh blood, but at this point, a quick death was more important. If only he would move closer.

Didn't the brat understand Conan's schedule?

His hand ached. A whisper of breath escaped his lips, and he relaxed his fingers. Slightly. His boots scraped the sidewalk as he neared the front steps, sidling around another row of trees. The stench threatened to choke him.

Conan swallowed hard, pushing through the sensation. Not real. Only a psychosomatic response to their pious attitudes. So Jean-Claude said. Of course, he wasn't here. He never took the hard jobs.

"Zeke, I told you to wait for me. You can't be outside alone."

Conan ducked behind a nearby shrubbery. A woman emerged from the house, her dark hair pulled back tightly, wearing exercise clothes that clung to her muscular figure. The brat scurried between the dogs, his face screwed into a pout.

"I want to go outside *now*. You didn't hafta change. You look okay like that."

Conan fought the urge to laugh. Zurina Vectorix Yamamoto

herself. Deadly in combat, but a bullet was a marvelous equalizer. Even for someone like her. Suddenly, the Victorian environment made sense. Naturally Mistress Zurina found comfort in the architecture of her own time period.

His lips curled into a sneer. The Vectorix harpy had always fancied herself a woman of taste. Never mind that she had been an unfit governess, hindering his development with her absurd morality. Aleron had succumbed, but his brother had always been weak. As weak as Grandfather Gabrel, who had fallen for Mistress Zurina's charms and relinquished his significant power in favor of absurd sentiment. How he maintained control over the Talamar House was beyond Conan's comprehension.

If only Jean-Claude hadn't specifically requested her live capture. But accidents happened all the time. Conan could hardly be blamed if he reacted in the heat of the moment.

The woman pressed her lips together. "Ezekiel Aleron, that isn't the-"

Conan straightened and whipped out the pistol. Aimed. Fired.

"Zeke, get down!"

CHAPTER SIX
BLACK EYE, PEAS

The crack of gunfire snapped through Melrose. Echoed through the high-security room. He dropped Jane's hand, staring at Akira. The other man straightened from his crouch beside her bed, his hands clenched into fists.

"The porch?"

Akira's eyes flared. *"Merde."*

Out the door. Akira five steps ahead of him. Up the basement stairs, two at a time. The soles of Melrose's wingtips scuffing on the hardwood. Sharp turn around the bannister, skidding on the worn red rug that covered the living room floor. Pushing through the dachshunds who scratched and barked at the front entrance.

Akira swung the front door open. *"S'il vous plaît Dieu. Zuri? Zeke!"*

Melrose followed him outside. Blood coated the porch in garish streaks, the metallic scent sharp in the humid summer air. The heavy form of a St. Bernard sprawled near the steps, mouth open, tongue lolling out. No expansive warmth in its eyes. A low growl drew Melrose's attention to a corner of the porch. The other St. Bernard crouched, teeth bared. Two dark eyes peered over the beast's broad back.

Melrose's heart sped. "Zeke?"

"I'm s'posed to stay here." His small hands trembled, nestled in the dog's brown and white coat. "Maman said. S'posed to stay here. For you."

"*Où est-elle?*" Akira crossed the distance in large bounds and knelt. One hand on the dog's muzzle, calming it with a few strokes. The other cupping Zeke's face, wiping away the tears with his thumb. "Zeke, where is she?"

The child gave a hiccupy sob. He uncurled his right hand from the coat, wafting shedded fur into the air, and pointed out into the street.

Melrose's stomach jumped. Zuri stood on the sidewalk, hands up on either side of her face, still in exercise clothes. Dark ponytail rain-slicked against her head. A pistol shoved against her temple, clutched by a man in a leather duster and broad-brimmed hat. A stern face and square jaw peeked out from under the hat.

Conan.

He glanced their way, his sharp face breaking into a gleaming smile. "Ah, I knew there was a reason I waited. So much better with an audience. Thank you, Mistress Zurina, for wasting your breath to distract me. Now you can die in front of your son, your bastard husband, and the traitor Thoth. A fitting end for the Vectorix princess."

She sighed slowly, her features forming a serene mask. The one Melrose had seen many times on the training mat. "So it seems.

Victory is yours. Although I doubt your master wants me dead."

"You struggled when I tried to capture you." Conan shrugged. "I had no choice."

Akira rose to his feet, his eyes fixed on his wife.

"Zeke?" He whispered. "When I give word, run to Uncle Melrose. Go inside. *Oui*?"

"*Oui*."

What word? Melrose barely restrained himself from speaking aloud. Zurina could fight capably. More than capably. But the barrel was pressed far too close, indenting the tan skin on her forehead.

No room for error.

His chest tightened. She had many gifts, but was hardly perfect. Melrose knew that better than anyone else.

God, please make her perfect.

Zuri's hand wavered slightly, her fingers curling down.

Akira leaped over the porch fence. "Zeke, now!"

Zuri grabbed Conan's wrists and twisted. Another gunshot echoed on the street, along with the crunch of broken bones. Swearing broke from Conan, and he tried to yank his arm away. Her leg shot out in a front kick that caught him in the left side.

"Uncle Melrose?" A hand tugged hard at his. Melrose spared a glance at Zeke, who looked up at him earnestly through black bangs. "Papa said go inside. He means it."

"Yes. Yes, small one." He scooped up the child, fur and all.

One more look at the street. Zuri held the gun now, Akira at her side. Both of them faced Conan, who clutched his mangled wrist in one hand. His brow drawn in a scowl beneath the hat.

"A clever trick. But do you really think I came alone?"

Five figures emerged from the trees lining the street, clothed in long coats and hats. Vampires. Not only in action, but in heart. Fully committed to darkness and just as deadly as Conan.

Akira's eyes narrowed, studying the figures intently. His expression turned to stone. Melrose knew that expression. Steeling himself to take their lives.

All of them pulled out pistols and aimed them at the couple. Conan smirked and nodded his head, water spilling off the brim of his hat. "Remember, slaves, Jean-Claude wants the princess alive. Kill the lab rat if you must." He afforded Zuri a last glance, holding up his hand. "I'll repay you for this later. Farewell, Mistress Zuri."

Conan backed up, then pivoted with a swoop of his coat. He almost pulled off the gesture, but then he crumpled, his good hand grasping his left side. He stumbled the rest of the way to a sleek black car down the street.

The vampires moved closer, circling Akira and Zuri. Their teeth bared, showing their fangs.

Akira gave his wife a sideways look. Lean muscles taut beneath the sweater and jeans. "A *partie*. Ready?"

"With you? Always." Her lips curled in a smirk.

Zeke gave a little giggle in his ear. "We can go in now, Uncle. Maman and Papa can fix this. Afterwards, they'll come inside. They always come back. Together."

"Now who is the smart one?" Melrose hefted Zeke into a better position, and reached for the door handle.

Behind him, more gunshots broke the calm. Then the solid blows and meaty sounds of flesh pummeling flesh. Echoing another time. When blood flowed over the altars, pouring down from the smashed reservoirs in the walls. His parents, pierced with the blades of Roman conquerors.

Blades that may as well have been in his hands. His traitorous words had struck them and their cabal down as much as the short swords. Ending the stranglehold of vampires on Alexandria.

Except for one.

Ramos.

Unbidden, the memories continued. A man, with the same light brown skin and tight curls, running into the room. His gray-blue eyes wide with shock. And anger.

Murderer. Betrayer. Outcast.

"Uncle? Inside?"

Bile rose in Melrose's throat. He could certainly miss this part of the struggle.

* * *

Plink. Plink-plink-plonk. Plink-plink-plonk.

Plink.

Her first piano recital. Age six. Did her fingers remember the keys? If not, her stomach certainly remembered the nerves. Even now it roiled and grumbled. Her mouth wet with saliva.

Afterwards, Mom had taken her out for onion rings and milkshakes. The cold, creamy sweetness mixed just right with the crisp, salty rings.

Hunger.

Jane's eyes popped open. Still the same room, lit with indirect bulbs and only a bed for furniture. Still hooked up to IVs, although both bags were nearly empty. Still alone.

Although she hadn't been. Not earlier. She touched a spot on the left side of the bed, the sheets soft and cool. Melrose had sat there, his dark eyes warm with caring. His fingers holding hers tightly.

But she had driven him away. Lucy had driven him away, accusing him of forgetting her. Of not loving her.

"You know he doesn't." The voice was hers, but lower with acid bitterness. The plinking sang off-key. "He still hasn't told you anything about these people or this place. About who he really is."

"Shut up! We never wanted to know." Jane pushed herself up in the bed, her teeth clenched. "We've only been here a few days. You need to back off. You're me and we love him, all right?"

"Yes, but we always wondered what he hid. Beneath your careless attitude, you wondered-"

"-why he would choose someone like me." Melrose was over two thousand years old. Dwarfing her forty-something age. It had taken her months to trust that he actually liked her, a rebellious Blood Kind eager to explore anything that kept her away from the stifling authority of the Paxena House and their Rules of Separation. "Look, you're me, and I'm hungry."

"Hmmm. Blood does sound good."

"No. It doesn't. I want real food." Jane shook her head and began prying at the needles in her hands and arms. Carefully probing the skin for release. Melrose always wanted to teach her nursing. As a Cryptaro, she had the intellect for it, but never the patience. Never wanted to be tied down to a career. As long as she had her cameras and the internet, she could work anywhere.

Even though she only really wanted to be where he was.

Lucy's voice grew fainter. "Imagine that life. Forced to tag along on his do-good adventures. He'd never let you be free to do what you want. Trapped in laboratories for long hours, hunched over microscopes—"

"As opposed to being hunched over my laptop for long hours, editing photos? You're a really bad debater. Wait, did I just insult myself?" Jane grimaced, gripping the tube. She slid the needle out quickly, before the pain could register. A tiny stream of blood squirted from the spot. Pressure. It needed pressure.

She bunched up a handful of sheet fabric and shoved it against the wound.

But it wasn't there. The puncture was gone, skin unmarked. "What on earth?"

Lucy was silent, drifting back into the tide of Jane's thoughts. All the better. She studied the spot, tracing it, then focused on the other tube. Slowly, she eased out that needle as well, resisting the urge to stop the blood flow.

A momentary spurt. Then new skin rose to the surface and filled the hole.

Panic hammered her chest. She could handle Lucy. Sort of. But this?

This needed Melrose.

Jane swung her legs over the side of the bed. Grabbing the mattress with her left hand, she settled her bare feet on the ground. The cold tile curled her toes. She should paint them with nail polish. Later.

She managed to stand, the ground shifting beneath her, as if on a leisurely boat ride. Jane set her jaw. Not a fun experience, but not unmanageable. She'd survived four hours on that fishing boat in Svalbard, just to get a shot of an iceberg under the moonlit sky.

One step. Then another, slapping her soles firmly on the ground. Plink. Plink-plink-plonk. Plink-plink-plonk.

She reached for the door, which was dark gray and even colder than the floor. Solid metal. Why?

To keep vampires in during detoxification. Melrose had explained all of this over dinner one night. Calamari and crusty bread in southern Italy. The salty brine-breeze off the water mingled with the flavors. He'd gone into detail about his methods of redeeming vampires, but she hadn't cared at the time. Or at least, not as much as she'd cared about drinking wine and kissing him.

"Basically, I was an idiot." Jane sighed. "Watch me not be able to open this."

The knob twisted beneath her hands of its own accord. Her breath caught and she tripped back, barely keeping erect. Either this was a new trick of her split mind, or-

"*Salut?*" The door swung open, revealing a tall, lean man with a thatch of unruly dark hair, a fine-boned, angular face, and eyes that were nearly black. Well, one eye. The other was covered with a plastic bag of—frozen peas?

Jane raised her eyebrows. "Who are you?"

His uncovered eye fixed on her, glinting intensely. Then, as if satisfied, it gleamed with good humor. "Ah, awake! *Bien, bien.* Jane?"

His words and his accent were French. Was that some kind of new language program in Japan? During her last visit, English and Chinese had been popular. Not that he couldn't learn French; it wasn't against the law.

"Yeah. I'm Jane." Her stomach growled.

"You need food." He held out his right hand, his thin lips broadening into a bright smile. His left hand still held the peas in place. "Akira Yamamoto. Your host here. You've met my wife, *oui?*"

A vague image of a strong-boned brunette in a corset and skirt filled her mind. Jane nodded, shaking his hand. "I think so."

"*Bien.* Come now. As you are awake, and need food, I will make you some." He beckoned her with one hand, then began walking upstairs. "*Excusez-moi*, but we had uninvited guests and I did not block my eye as I should have."

"Right. Block your eye." Jane followed him up the stairs, the cool cement prickling her skin. Light glowed through the square entrance at the top. "Does that happen a lot?"

"No. But sometimes, I am careless."

The doorway opened into a front hall with hardwood floors and cream walls. Rain spattered outside through the inlaid glass door and rectangular windows on either side.

"You should have told me!" A woman's voice, alto and fierce.

Jane glanced to the left, towards the sound. A red rug lined a room with an overstuffed dark blue couch and easy chair. The woman, Zuri, paced in front of a flat screen TV, wearing tight exercise clothes splattered with brownish-red stains. Another voice answered her in a calm baritone, his words too soft to hear.

Jane knew that voice. Knew the face of the man perched on the edge of the couch, his elbows resting on his knees, fingers steepled. Still wearing his favorite ensemble of dress pants and crisp button-down.

Jane turned to Akira. "What's going on?"

Akira looked over her head and sighed. "Family discussion. Give them time. Come, I will make whatever you want."

"Family?" Jane tore her herself away from the scene. It seemed like Melrose had kept secrets from a lot of people. The old resentment burned in her chest. No! She couldn't give Lucy—the worst part of herself—a foothold. "You're all family?"

"He is her godfather." He shrugged. "And her primary doctor. *C'est compliqué.*"

"Got it. Complicated." Jane opened her mouth with more questions, and swallowed back more saliva. Food. She wanted it. "Can you make onion rings and vanilla milkshakes?"

Akira's smile widened. *"Oui."*

* * *

Zuri's eyes burned into his skull.

Not literally. Otherwise Melrose would have died decades ago. His goddaughter had a rare but fierce temper. Only those deemed close enough were even allowed to see any negative emotions beneath her peaceful surface.

He'd seen her face twisted with anger and disappointment more often than anyone. Not always directed at him. Merely needing a sounding board.

"I don't understand. She meant enough that you married her, and yet..." Zuri's voice trailed off, and she swallowed. "Yet you kept her from me."

Melrose seized the pause. "Zurina, I was trying to protect you."

"Protect me?" Hurt flashed in her hazel eyes. "By keeping secrets?"

His shoulders slumped and he rubbed his forehead. Of all the words that could have slipped out of his mouth. He could only blame the recent turmoil for addling his mind. "You know that isn't what I meant. Of course I keep secrets. But I'm not going to shut you out."

"That's what you did." Zurina exhaled. Her anger fading into deep sadness.

Guilt sank into the pit of his stomach, halting any excuses. Not that there were any rational reasons for his decisions. Rationality and Jane didn't belong in the same category. "She didn't want anyone to know. Not at first. She is a free spirit in that regard."

He pressed his fingertips to his forehead. The couch shifted next to him as Zuri sat down. She spoke quietly, "Yet you're married to her."

"Yes. I love her. She loves me. After a year, we both finally admitted it." A chuckle escaped him. "Around her, I don't feel so old. She's so focused on the present. Every moment, every taste of food, every sunset. I've never met anyone like that who I could tolerate for more than ten minutes."

"Heart-warming, as always." Humor warmed her voice, and she nudged his shoulder with hers. "She's Cryptaro strain. What's her savant aptitude?"

Melrose's lips twitched, picturing Jane at their first meeting. Frowning intently at him through the lens of her camera, as if willing the lighting to improve. "Mechanical intelligence. She has superior skill in electronics and anything with intricate parts. I've seen her study a new camera for ten minutes and be able to use it, take it apart, and put it back together without any missing pieces. She has an exceptional mind for detail and remarkable hand-eye coordination."

Zuri placed her hand on his arm. When he looked up, her eyes were compassionate as well as sad. "Then Jean-Claude took her. Uncle, we could have been looking for her. We could have helped you find her."

"I had already lost her." Melrose pressed his fingertips harder together. "I couldn't bear losing anyone else."

"Akira and I are used to being targets. You saw how we handled ourselves today. We've been doing this for eighty years."

He turned to face her. Studying her features. Seeing a tiny toddler, barely able to walk and speak, stumbling towards him with her mouth curved in a shy smile. Perfect. But so fragile. And somehow, through Vir's emotional breakdown and neglect, entrusted to him. "You're a parent. You have Zeke. You have to understand that I couldn't subject you to that danger."

She paused, then nodded. "I know. It's one of the reasons we settled here, in Quebec City. To try to give Zeke a normal upbringing, as much as possible."

"Admirable. You are both doing an excellent job."

Zuri's cheeks flushed, and her lips finally tilted up into that same shy smile. "I had a good example."

"A miracle, considering that I didn't."

She moved closer to him, loose strands of hair brushing his shoulder. Fighting had always defeated any attempts to contain her wavy locks. "Any idea what Jean-Claude's plans were for her?"

"Akira and I were discussing it before the attack."

"I noticed the scars on her skin. Occult?"

Melrose shook his head. "No. Akira confirmed it. And she isn't possessed. Only mentally troubled by the event, which is understandable. But in some way, her faith held her together."

Zuri nodded. "So, what of the scars? What else could she be used for?"

"An excellent question. One we only have five days to discover. No, four."

"Four days?"

He rubbed his forehead. "Until Quebec City falls to blood. At least, that's what her alter ego said. Lucy must have formed during torture, a distancing mechanism. I thought it was Jean-Claude's hyperbole brainwashed into her, but considering Conan's arrival, I think we should prepare for the worst."

Zuri's shoulders loosened. "Conan didn't give us much trouble outside, Uncle. Only his usual smugness and bold words. Akira and I dealt with his people easily, for the most part."

"Did you take anyone alive?"

"No. They were too committed to the cause. We had no choice but to defend ourselves and kill them. As for Conan, I couldn't-" Zuri clasped her hands in her lap. Unwilling to voice the reasons they both knew all too well. Reasons that went deeper than merely her part in raising Conan among the Talamars. "Still, it was a successful skirmish. Plus, we have Jane here, and we can protect her from any other intruders."

Melrose gave her a level stare. "What of Jean-Claude?"

"If he wants to retrieve her, he'll have to do it in person. We both know he rarely gets involved in attacks."

"Yes. But his actions make no sense. He could have killed Jane in captivity, and instead he released her."

"Oh? I thought you found her."

He leaned forward, resting his head in his hands.

"Yes. But all the more, I wonder why he allowed her to roam free in the first place."

"People can make mistakes, Uncle. Even evil people."

An image of Jane's scarred body flashed in his mind. "Yes. But Jean-Claude's plans are never straightforward. He uses mistakes as part of the whole."

The marks on Melrose's wife were not a mistake.

CHAPTER SEVEN
THE ANATOMY OF ONION RINGS

Akira didn't have a kitchen. He had a space station.

Solid cement paved the large rectangle of space, with thick rubber mats in front of the deep double sink and the stainless steel island that ran down the center of the room. A large, six-burner gas stove stood across from the counter, and in a corner sat an industrial refrigerator. All of the other space was filled with steel cabinets.

Jane didn't know if she should pour herself a glass of water, or wait for the mother ship to arrive. The percussion in her mind swished and crashed in response. For some reason, her mind decided that a mash-up of all the drum solos she had ever heard was a great idea.

"Jane! *Fais attention!*"

She started. "What?"

Akira pointed to the fryer in front of her. The one that held onion rings and was about to bubble over with oil. Jane bit her lip with her sharp incisor, drawing blood and a burst of pain. "Oh, crap! What do I do?"

He stood in front of three other fryers a few feet down, managing them expertly. "Turn it down. Sift! Sift!"

The snare drums beat out a rapid pit-patting sound, like rain on a tin roof. "Sift? Do you mean 'drain'? Take the basket out?"

"*Oui, oui*! The rack!"

"Got it!" Jane grabbed the handles of the basket and pulled it out, resting it on the rack suspended above the oil to drain. Slick yellowish drops spat out of the gloop, sizzling on her skin. "Ouch! Okay. What next?"

"Next, wait for draining." His baskets were already sitting in their racks, filled with golden-brown onion rings. Enough to feed at least twenty people. Apparently, being fed in his kitchen involved work. At least she didn't have to clean up. Apparently there were former vampires in the area who cleaned houses as a way to earn income.

"Got it." She wiped her hands on the white apron tied around her waist, wincing as the burn touched the cloth.

Akira glanced over at her. "You are hurt?"

"Just a little." She held up her hand ruefully. The burn was already fading, along with the puncture from her sharp tooth. Jane was almost getting used to the rapid healing, as ridiculous as that seemed.

He nodded, tilting his head to the side. "Hm. Convenient, the healing. A gift from God."

"Sure, I guess." Jane shrugged. "Or a curse from Conan and Jean-Claude and whoever else messed with me over the last five years."

She didn't remember. Those were Lucy's experiences, and as

much as Jane wanted a whole brain, she didn't want it enough to deal with the insecurity, fear, and other, far uglier, emotions that lurked in the dark corners of her mind. "Are we ready?"

"*Oui*. Nearly. All we must do is package these up, and set them out on the side porch. I called a friend from the church to take them for an event tonight." Akira pulled out two pairs of plastic gloves from a drawer, along with foil-lined paper bags, and set them on the counter with a smile. "Very quick, I promise."

Jane rolled her eyes, but found herself smiling back. There was something in his friendly demeanor that blew right through any complaints, and made her just as eager to package the food as he was. Well, and he'd let her sample the first batch, along with a fresh vanilla milkshake. Besides, it was fun to make something with her hands that would benefit others, especially after being stuck in a bed for the last few days.

Before that, we were slaves. You remember that too, don't you, dear Jane?

"Not right now I don't." The bass drums pounded out a steady beat.

Akira glanced at her, folding over a sack and sealing it. "Your mind is loud?"

"*Oui*. I mean yes. That's one way of putting it." She wrapped a handful of onion rings in wax paper. "So, I didn't realize you were a chef. When did that happen?"

"After I escaped from the *laboratoire*, I wandered. Trying to comprehend what I saw and what I could do. I wasn't born Blood Kind, so I did not comprehend that either. But in grace, I found shelter at a *hôpital*—hospital in France, and they knew of Blood Kind. Transfusions cost money, so I needed a job. I washed dishes at a restaurant." He smiled sheepishly. "1920s. Almost no Japanese there. If I spoke Japanese, the chef threw things at me. So, I learned French."

Jane nodded. With his sleeves rolled up, she could see the white scars criss-crossing Akira's arms and disappearing beneath the fabric near his elbows. A lot more scars than hers, though without the blood in the centers.

"You said you could do things. What kinds of things?"

"I shouldn't, but-" He paused, shooting a look at the kitchen entrance. Melrose and Zuri must still be talking. "I'll show. Step back. This counter, it is not sealed—glued to the floor."

"Okay…"

Akira's smile faded into focus, and he placed his hands beneath the metal island. It shuddered. Slowly, it began to lift off the floor. Jane raised her eyebrows. Soon the entire piece floated a foot in the air.

No, not floated. The sweat lining Akira's face showed exactly who was responsible. With a grunt, he carefully lowered the island once more.

The percussion switched to a solo, with a ba-boom-crash!

"Wow. So you're a Vectorix? Jean-Claude liked to use them for their hyper-senses." *And because they could snap men's bones like they were twigs. Women and children too-* Jane shunted away Lucy's voice. Not now.

Akira wiped his palms on his full-body apron. "Vectorix

blood. And Cryptaro. And Talamar. All three blood curse strains."

He sagged on the cold metal surface for a moment, his face three shades paler than it was before.

Jane reached towards him hesitantly. "You all right?"

"Three strains means three times the physical toll," said a soft alto voice from the doorway. Zuri gave a smile that didn't reach her eyes, and she strode over to her husband. "Three times the side effects. You, *tomodachi*, certainly have many effects from that fight today. Did you take another transfusion? What are you thinking, showing off?"

He pushed himself up from the counter and snaked an arm around her waist, pressing a kiss to her forehead. "Only being a good host, *ma belle*."

"Mmhm. Naturally." She sighed and leaned into Akira's embrace. "Well, Uncle and I are at peace."

"*Tres bien*. Now you can help us package the onion rings!"

Jane gestured at the counter. "Actually, I'm done. Voila."

A line of ten bags of onion rings marched in front of her on the counter. Her fingers always knew what to do before her mind. Extreme kinesthetic intelligence, something that ran in her family's strain of the blood curse. Along with the sensory disconnects. At least her musical hallucinations weren't as bad as her father's. He could only communicate through singing words instead of speaking them.

"Up to your old tricks? Good." The voice was low and brisk.

A shiver trickled through her spine, but Jane only faced Melrose with a smirk. "Was that a compliment?"

His dark eyes glinted, showing clear relief. "Merely an observation."

"I see."

Melrose entered the kitchen, approaching her, but stopping just short. She lingered over his figure, enjoying the way his clothes were smoothly tailored to his frame. The line of his chiseled jaw, and how it set just right in his defined features. She was married to him.

Her husband's lips quirked. "Inspecting my attire?"

"You could say that." With Lucy and her horrible memories out of the way, other ideas filled Jane's mind. Ideas that didn't involve clothing. "You've passed."

"As have you. Although I never took you as one who wore robes." Melrose's expression hinted at moments from their honeymoon. Heat zipped through Jane's veins. Then he turned to Akira. "Is Zeke still resting?"

"*Oui.* Maybe for another thirty minutes."

Zuri disentangled herself from Akira's arms. "Then I'm going to take a shower before he wakes."

"*C'est excellente.*" Akira gave his wife a favorable glance that trailed over her figure. "But showers can be very dangerous places, so I think I will put this food on the porch and then join you, *mon amour.*"

"Always the gentleman." She smiled at him over her shoulder.

Those two had the right angle. Jane turned back to Melrose. "What about you?"

"Regrettably, we should move to another location as well."

"Oh?" She put her hands on her hips and closed the distance between them. Breathing in his warm, clean scent. "And why is that regrettable?"

Her husband exhaled. "You are due for another examination."

The onion rings and milkshake lurched in her stomach. Her shoulders slouched, and the drums returned to the frantic, rain-on-a-tin-roof part of the cycle. "You know how to show a girl a good time, Melrose Durante."

* * *

"Why don't *you* have to be naked?"

Melrose tried not to smile. An impossible task when his wife sat on the examination table in the stark room, staring at him archly, her soft lips quirking. "First, you're not naked. You're wearing an examination gown. Second-"

"I might as well be naked. I'm not wearing anything underneath this." She crossed her slim, pale legs.

His skin and blood jolted into a fury of tingles. Sensations Melrose had never considered he could feel, until Jane walked into his life. One slow breath in, and breath out. He needed to think. "I believe that was your choice. I gave you the option of dressing according to your comfort level."

"Maybe I'd feel more comfortable if you were naked."

Melrose blinked. Trying to find words. As usual, she had a disturbingly effective way of reminding him of the basic facts in a situation. Facts that parts of him were quite willing to follow to a natural conclusion. This examination room had even been recently sterilized.

No. He clamped down on the wayward thoughts. Jane remained psychologically unstable. In addition, her incisors were still sharp. Never mind the effect physical stimulus could have on her delicate system.

"You all right? I'd hate to think I was distracting you."

"Merely collecting my thoughts." Melrose let out another long, slow breath. In front of him were examination gloves. He needed to put them on. A simple process, and one he had done countless times, even in earlier instances when he'd examined his wife while she was unconscious.

But right now, the latex seemed an unwanted barrier to her skin.

He cleared his throat and turned to face Jane. Her eyes watched him, sharp and expectant. Beautiful green eyes. "It has been confirmed on multiple occasions that your tissues heal rapidly from any injury, leaving no scar. However, that is incongruous with the scars that already mark your body."

"So the scars must have come before the super-healing kicked in, and they might even be part of whatever Jean-Claude did to increase my tissue regeneration."

"Correct." Melrose's smile widened. He stepped away from the counter and cabinets, the only other furnishing in the small space. "As of yet, medical science hasn't discovered any known element in standard human DNA that can be altered to effect this change."

She nodded, not even flinching as he gently touched the scars on her arms. Only a tremble in her lips revealed the true sensitivity of the wounds. "Which means he must have messed with the Cryptaro strain of the blood curse in my DNA."

A different warmth spread through him, this one a potent affection starting in his brain. For all her earthiness, Jane had the same intellectual gifts of any Cryptaro, and around him, no censorship in sharing them. His fingers lingered on the soft underside of her arm. "Precisely."

"I can be precise, on occasion." She reached out for his shirt. Likely to pull him towards her onto the table.

Melrose couldn't think of a single reason to resist. Still, his mind kept working. "The question is, why? What purpose did Jean-Claude have? What missions did he send you on?"

A wall of darkness dulled her eyes, and she jerked her arm back. "What's that to you?"

Lucy. No, he needed to get out of the habit of using her dissociation as an excuse. Jane had always had sudden lapses of emotion and separation. Her trauma only made that worse. Melrose forced himself to keep calm. "I'm your husband and a doctor. I want to understand what happened to you."

"Well, I don't." She pushed back on the vinyl-cushioned table. "The last thing I want is to give her control. She's a bitch." Melrose raised his eyebrows, and she continued. "Yes, I know she's part of me and that makes me a bitch. I don't want to deal with that. I'm out of there. I'm safe." Jane sighed, and curled her legs up underneath her. "I want to be here, not there."

Melrose hazarded a step closer to her, pulling off the gloves. Jane had always appreciated skin-to-skin contact. "I know. But if you don't remember, I can't help you. I need to know what happened."

She opened her mouth, then shut it. Her lips pruned into a scowl. "And what about you? You want to know what happened? Jean-Claude had a lot to say about you. Thoth. I remember that name. You used it at our wedding. I knew you were Egyptian, from old world Alexandria. I didn't know you massacred your family."

His muscles seized. The images from earlier surged through his mind again. Blood on the pagan altars. Ramos staring at him in horror and hatred.

Melrose swallowed. Ramos should have died then. Not been shut up in prison while Melrose fruitlessly tried to dissuade him from vampirism with reason. Logic. Prayer. Nothing had worked. It had only fed Ramos' rage.

Rage that burned fiercer as the centuries passed.

"Melrose?" He started. Jane was glaring at him. "You're doing it again. Hiding things from me."

"So I believe that puts us on equal footing."

She folded her arms across her chest. "Fine. I guess it does." His temples throbbed with dull pain. Melrose reached for a fresh pair of gloves. Either way, Jane needed to be examined. "I'll make this brief. You won't need to endure my company any more than necessary."

"Right. Because that's why I kept these rings on. I hate your company. Great logic."

"Your current attitude belies your words, and your logic."

He shut his eyes and rubbed his forehead. *God, I can't do this.*

Not after the fight that morning and then the conversation with Zuri. Another tailspin into emotions was the exact opposite of ideal. Couldn't Jane be a little more rational? These games were absurd when all he wanted to do was help her.

"Melrose?" Her voice had softened. Melrose opened his eyes to see her picking at her short strands of hair. Her face fragile with anxiety. "Are you going to leave?"

He breathed out a thin stream of air. Took care to gentle his voice. "No. Although-"

"It's hard. I'm difficult. I know." Jane pressed her lips together. "I'm...sorry."

"So am I. For all that has happened to you." He swallowed. "And for lacking patience."

"It's not easy for you."

"I didn't think it would be." He left off the gloves, instead lightly outlining her scars with a fingertip.

She leaned over to him. A habit he once knew how to interpret. Was it still true? Melrose eased onto the table and gathered her into his arms. Expecting Lucy.

His wife's muscles slowly unwound, melting into his embrace. When was the last time anyone had held her?

"We'll survive this, Jane."

She sighed. "At least until everyone dies. Because of me."

"Because of you?" Melrose kept his voice low, stroking her hair. She needed to feel safe.

"That's what Jean-Claude said. 'You're not a complete imbecile, Conan. This pretty toy is the key. My fool of a brother finally made a mistake. It will cost him everything.' That's what he said." She winced. "I don't understand. I heal. How could that be a bad thing?"

"I don't know. But you'll be here, safe, until we find out."

"...okay."

Jane's words barely penetrated the haze that deadened his senses and accelerated his thoughts into a storm.

She would be here. But he wouldn't.

Ramos had gone too far.

CHAPTER EIGHT
ILL MET BY CANDLELIGHT

"Stay away!"

The scream ripped from Jane's throat. Her fingers gripped the blanket in front of her, yanking it up to her chin and over her head.

If she hid, he couldn't find her. He couldn't bleed her wounds again with his merciless razor and bright-toothed smile. Her lungs heaved against her chest, squeezing in and out like a bellows.

My perfect weapon.

Not Lucy. No, the voice was a memory, and the memory held only needles stabbing her skin, pushing dark liquid beneath her veins. A warm laugh, delighting in her screams. Feeding off the torment, his words scraping at the edge of her mind. Trying to force a way in.

Jean-Claude.

A violin screeched in her mind, setting her teeth on edge. As if this couldn't get any worse.

"Our Father, who art in heaven…" Jane muttered the prayer slowly. As a child, the 'our Fathers' were bred into her by the priest and the catechism teachers. It was only in captivity that she learned to relish the meaning of each word.

"...the kingdom, the power, and the glory forever. Amen."
She rubbed her eyes, then blinked. Trying to glean what light she
could beneath the covers.

It wasn't the bed in the basement. It was twice as large, with
soft sheets that cocooned her in a safe nest. But suddenly, the
tight swaddle of cloth threatened to suffocate her. Jane shoved off
the bedclothes, kicking her legs out. Bare legs. She wore shorts
and a loose men's shirt.

Melrose's.

"Sorry, Melrose-" No point. Jane had only been married to
Melrose a year before her kidnapping, but that was long enough
to know he slept like the dead.

She shuddered. Bad analogy.

A second violin joined the first, their jagged, discordant notes
shrieking against each other.

Jane felt for the space next to her. Empty.

"Melrose? Melrose!" He should be there. After the failed examination, he'd carried her in his arms to his bedroom and spent
the evening with her. No pressure to do anything or say anything.
Just quiet time in his arms, sometimes listening to music, other
times the sound of his voice as he read aloud from various
favorite books and favorite poems. Bringing up memories of their
time in Venice and Tuscany, wandering through the markets and side
streets. No destination in mind. Life had seemed so simple then.

She'd married the founder and leader of the Houses of the
Dead. Life could never be simple.

Jane rolled over, her eyes confirming what her fingers already knew. The violin cacophony spiraled into her stomach with a lurch.

Melrose was gone.

* * *

Retracing Jane's movements was the first step.

Melrose shrugged deeper into his long coat, light enough to withstand the summer heat, but substantial enough to protect him from any outside contaminants. With Jane around, his compulsions lessened. But he couldn't take her here.

No one needed to come along.

Darkness cloaked the streets. The vampire hours. Although Akira and Zuri had assured him that Quebec City had been cleared of vampires months before. No doubt Vir Vectorix had something to do with that. The lead enforcer still attempted to care for his estranged daughter, even centuries after abandoning her to others.

Yet Jean-Claude hunted. And when he hunted, even the Blood Kind enforcers wouldn't be enough. Much less Akira and Zuri, no matter how skilled they were against a handful of vampires.

Not while Zuri persisted in hiding.

Melrose stopped in the alley where he'd first encountered Jane. He exhaled slowly, trying to recall any important details. A marked skill of his wife. But their time in the exam room had proven she was in no condition to help him.

As usual, in the end he had to work alone.

He scanned the ground. Something glinted in the garbage and muck around the crate where Jane had sat. Drawing him closer, despite the dirt and the dumpster nearby.

A white card stuck out of the grime, coated in questionable brownish smears. Melrose reached into his pocket for a tissue and picked up the card, sealing his nostrils against the sour odor of old beer and rotten food.

"Let no one doubt I care."

He studied the small rectangle in the dim light. An ideal time to have a Vectorix, with their acute senses. No matter. Anyone could squint.

A business card, with a priest's name on the front. Girard.

"Trying to clear your conscience *before* sinning?" Melrose rolled his eyes. "Because that's how it works, Jane."

He pictured the stubborn tilt of her head, her raised eyebrows, as she readied a comeback. Always something flippant and seemingly shallow, but with a sharp edge of truth that set him back. Why was he here, in the filth of this alley, instead of back in bed with her?

"This is what leadership is."

Melrose wrapped the card in a protective layer of tissues. It was Saturday, and according to the card, there was a Mass service.

It had been a long time.

* * *

70

You don't belong here. You're a danger.

"Shut up." Jane shoved her pillow over her head, burying her face in the mattress. In Melrose's arms, Lucy retreated into the farthest corners of her mind.

Without him, the cracked part of her mind surfaced and wouldn't leave her alone.

You'll kill them all.

A groan escaped her. "Is that a threat?"

"No. A fact that you keep overlooking. Why do you think I'm still here?" There was that voice. Almost Jane's, but lower and laden with venom. Only this time, it carried an undertone of resignation.

"Because a psychotic vampire kidnapped and brutally tortured me." Jane rolled out of the bed, her feet slapping the bare hardwood floor. She groped the bedside table for a light. Her fingers touched the thin wax pillar of a candle, stuck in a metal holder with a curved plate at the bottom and a handle at one side.

Butterfly wings fluttered in her heart. Of course. Melrose always preferred soft candle light to modern conveniences. Romantic, even if he called it an 'irrational vestige of his old age.' His eyes still melted like dark chocolate when they saw her across a candlelit room.

Why wasn't he here?

Jane felt around for the matches that would certainly be there. She carefully lit the wick and grabbed the handle, then crept through the room, along the narrow path between the dresser and the bed, towards the adjoining bathroom. Maybe Melrose had some kind of sleeping meds.

"Considering what he did to his family, he probably has a dozen. Only way he sleeps through the night." Lucy's voice dripped acid, echoed by a dramatic, off-key upstroke on the violin. Jane pressed her lips together.

She needed to see a shrink. Badly.

The small flame cast ghostly patterns on the white walls. Not even a picture or a postcard broke up the monotony. Hadn't she made him some prints of her photos? What happened to them?

Didn't he want to remember her?

She stepped into the cool-tiled bathroom. A tub with a shower on the right side and a sink on the left, with drawers beneath and mirrored cabinets at eye level. Jane turned to the left. The dim light cast her reflection in ghoulish shadows.

A chill trickled down her spine.

He bathed our scars in red. A memory flashed in her mind. Face down on a pillow, the downy fluff making her nose twitch and her throat thicken with mucous. Leather straps binding her wrists and arms horizontal on either side of her and her ankles to edge of the mattress.

"Such soft, white skin." Jean-Claude's voice was gentle with admiration, his fingertips stroking down her cheek and bare shoulder. "In my day, you would have made a pretty barbarian slave girl from the north. Something bought for my dearest, perhaps. She might have even kept you alive as a prize."

His fingers found the grooves on her back and shoved down hard, grinding arcs of pain into her nerves. Jane gasped, clutching her hands into fists. It never got easier. Never ended.

"Too bad...you messed me up. What's that...say about...you?"

Jean-Claude's breath whispered in her ear. "That I'm willing to make any sacrifice to see my family avenged. Even tarnish a slave." A breathy chuckle escaped him. "Your screams are charming. Let's see if you can reach a new decibel, shall we?"

"Go to-"

Needles shoved into her flesh, black holes of piercing agony that overloaded her senses. *God, please, help me!*

"Help me! I don't want to kill them!"

"Kill who?" A high-pitched voice. Zeke. "Fred, no!"

A warm tongue rasped her cheeks, and dog breath clogged her nostrils. Soft, short fur pressed beneath her fingers. She opened her eyes to fluorescent bathroom lights and two bright-eyed dachshunds. Behind them, Zeke crouched next to the St. Bernard, his small body on equal height with hers. Because she was kneeling. Her knees throbbed on the hard tile. Had she fallen?

The candle! She glanced around. The short stick was snapped in two next to the metal plate. No flame. Her chest exhaled a large breath. At least she hadn't burned the house down.

A cold comfort. Jane would kill them all soon, thanks to Jean-Claude's sick little experiments.

"Are you okay?" Zeke pinched his bottom lip between his fingers. "Maman and Papa will be here soon. Papa's just doing a tra-trus-"

"Transfusion?"

"One of those. I don't like them, but Maman says they're important."

"Yes, but only if you want to live." A smile twitched her lips. The boy reminded Jane of when her baby sister had first learned about the blood curse, and asked about the strange things with tubes her big sister and parents did a couple of times a week. The blood curse manifested around the age of five.

Jean-Claude will kill them if you fail.

"Lies," she snapped. "Empty threats. We both know that. *I* know that! We need to find Melrose and tell him what happened!"

Lucy retreated, but this time with an odd satisfaction.

We'll see how that goes. He won't believe you.

The violins whined down to a low minor key. How long had Jane been scared of a mere man? A vicious killer who enjoyed blood and occult torture, but a man.

Renewed energy filled her muscles.

Zeke stared at her, his fingers clutching the back of the St. Bernard's neck scruff. "What's a threat?"

"I am." Jane pushed her palms into the tile and rose to her feet, her knees creaking. "But it doesn't have to be that way."

Not when she was married to the world's foremost physician. She brushed past Zeke.

"Where are you going?"

"To find my husband."

CHAPTER NINE
HAIL, BROTHER OF MINE

"I'm sorry, you just missed Mass."

The priest met Melrose halfway down the long, carpeted aisle that connected the tall wooden doors to the raised dais framed in an alcove of narrow stone archways. An ornate altar rested on the dais, festooned with a filigreed dome and a statue of the crucifix. Stained glass windows adorned the high walls, the saints and other figures within the panes staring down at the empty pews and kneelers.

St. Luke's Church of Our Savior. Melrose may have left the Catholic church for his own reasons, but he could never fault the beauty of their architecture.

He curved his mouth into a faint smile. "That isn't why I'm here, Father Girard. I need to speak with you about a confession."

"Oh. Would you like to make one?" The priest's face settled into a comforting expression, crow's feet deepening around his pale green eyes. "I'm happy to listen."

Also unnecessary. Melrose paused. Directness would be best. "No, thank you. I haven't since the Reformation."

The priest raised sparse white eyebrows. "The Reformation? That's-you're-"

"A Blood Kind."

"Not a vampire?" Girard flinched, his shoulders hunching. So, Jane had visited here. Likely as Lucy. Had anyone else? Vampires had a fractious relationship with the Catholic church. It had long been a force against them—but also, a tool easily corrupted.

Like all forms of organized religion.

Melrose pulled out his wallet, making every move clear. He slipped out his medical identification card and held it up, opening his mouth for a moment to reveal his flat, normal teeth. "Be at peace, Father. Melrose Durante. Registered with Cryptaro House."

Technically the king of all Blood Kind, although this was hardly the time to flash full credentials. He only created the title to satisfy politicians and grant Blood Kind sovereign status within their chosen nations. Self-regulation was preferred over government regulation.

Even if it meant far too much paperwork on Melrose's desk, as well as mandatory attendance at state functions.

The priest glanced at the card, relaxing. "I see. Very well. I've learned there are many of you in this area."

"Humans? Yes. The planet is full of them."

Father Girard paused, clearing his throat and pulling at his tight, round collar. "Well, no. That is, that's very true, and I've done a little research on your condition. Very sad, the blood curse, really, and ah, I meant no disrespect regarding your status. It seems I have much to learn."

"Of course not. None taken." Melrose injected his voice with as much warmth as he could muster. God forgive him. Most humans knew nothing about vampires or Blood Kind. It made life simpler to label their condition as merely another blood disorder. But the priest had obviously endured a difficult time with Lucy, and no wonder, considering her volatility.

Volatility that came at the most inconvenient time. In a month the annual summit of the Houses of the Dead was scheduled. And yet, Jane needed to heal mentally and physically from her trauma. He should contact Gabrel Talamar. Zuri wouldn't be pleased, but careful maneuvering could maintain their separation. Gabrel was still the best psychologist and counselor of the Blood Kind.

Melrose sighed. And to think, he had fallen in love with Jane for her independence, for her freedom from the politics of the Blood Kind. Now she was another problem on his list.

He pushed the thought away. Also unkind. Jane was his wife, and he would make time to ensure she received the best care. If she hadn't married him, she wouldn't even be in this position. She wouldn't be a target for Ramos.

Another thought to cast aside before it stung any further.

"Mr. Durante? How can I help you?"

Melrose gave his temples a final rub before glancing at the priest. "My apologies, Father. I'm inquiring after a woman who would have come into your church. A vampire, actually, seeking confession."

Another faint flinch. Yes, Jane had come here. "Vampires rarely seek confession."

"This woman is hardly typical, and she is in the process of rehabilitation. I believe she would have called herself Lucy." No verbal affirmation from the priest, but the tightening of his brows said enough. "She was—is—Catholic and holds great store in confessions. I need to know what she said to you."

Father Girard drew himself up to his full height, several inches taller than Melrose. Not that it was any great accomplishment. "I'm afraid I can't do that. The seal of confession covers her words."

Ah yes, that damned seal. Another reason Jane took comfort in confession. She said that, besides absolution, she had peace in the sanctity of that vow. Melrose exhaled slowly, willing himself to remain calm. "Her full name is Lucille Jane Durante. She is my wife. Currently her mind is fractured, and at this stage in her healing, she doesn't want to dwell on the past. However, what happened to her as a vampire is critical to saving the lives of many. I need to know what she said to you."

"I'm sorry. I can't do that." The priest set his jaw. "She confessed in absolute confidence. Now, if you returned with her here and she released me from the seal, then I could tell you. It might be easier than her speaking of it herself."

A shadow passed over the priest's face. Worry stirred within Melrose, combined with a flicker of jealousy. Jane couldn't speak to him of anything that happened to her, but Lucy had revealed it to a priest? What sort of marriage was this?

One where they both enjoyed keeping their own lives. Even at the risk of alienating each other.

He breathed in, trying to center his thoughts—and a sharp,

coppery tang filled his mouth. Melrose's heart stopped. Only one man enjoyed blood so much he used it as a fragrance.

Shoes clicked unevenly on the stone floor behind him.

"If the priest won't help you—and they never do—then you could always ask me, brother." Jean-Claude. Melrose turned, facing his brother's gray-blue eyes, winsome face, and skin the same shade of brown as his own. "After all, I had the pleasure of inflicting all sorts of pain on her."

Melrose clenched his hands into fists.

"Hello, Ramos."

*   *   *

As it turned out, Zuri and Akira both spoke Japanese. At least when they wanted to have conversations no one could understand. From Zeke's expression, the kid was as clueless as she was.

But Jane could read body language. Zuri's arms were crossed and her mouth pinched tight. She'd switched back to the corset, blouse, and skirt. Probably the clothing from her birth era. Jane's father still refused to wear anything but overalls and genuine leather boot`s. No zippers and no plastics.

She began edging towards the door in the front entrance. Asking Zuri and Akira for help had been a formality. No one could really keep her inside the house. Not if she ran fast enough.

"It won't work." A hand grabbed at the jeans she'd changed into. Zeke looked up at her earnestly. "They're both really fast. Especially when they're protecting people. It's what they do."

"Yeah? How long have they been taking in people?"

His face scrunched up in thought. "A long time. Decades and decades. Although Uncle Melrose says Maman has a das-destriny."

"Destriny? You mean destiny?"

Zeke nodded with a yawn. "Yeah, that one. He won't say anything more."

"I bet he won't." She leaned against the wall. One thing Melrose seemed really good at was keeping secrets. As good as she was at avoiding anything serious. Anything that would threaten her freedom.

Akira and Zuri's voices were quiet now, and he held her hands in his. Her frozen face had thawed into love and understanding. The trust in their expressions made Jane's heart tighten. She'd thought it was a good sign when Melrose never fought with her during their year of dating and year of marriage. Rarely a single disagreement.

Because they never dealt with anything together. She rolled her wedding ring and engagement ring around her finger. Zuri and Akira didn't even wear their bands most of the time. Yet, there were no secrets.

"*Oui, oui.*" Akira kissed Zuri, then turned to Jane. "We'll take you to Melrose. You said you might know where he is?"

Jane nodded, standing up straight and shoving deeper into her hoodie. "Yeah. The priest gave me a business card after confessing, and it's gone. It probably fell out when I was running with-" Her throat swelled. "-running. Melrose would retrace all those steps. And anyway, he knows I like to confess."

Humor glinted in Zuri's hazel eyes. "I see. All right, I'll grab the emergency transfusions. Akira-"

"I will contact the Vectorix and tell them to expect Zeke." Akira squeezed his wife's hands one final time, brushing strands of hair out of her face. "*Je t'aime.*"

"*Je t'aime.* Keep your eyes open." Zuri turned to Zeke. "Go and pack a bag. And a blanket and pillow."

He yawned again. "Not. Sleepy."

"Of course you're not. But you might be when you get to the Vectorix station." She scooped him up in her arms, rubbing her nose against his. "Choose some books too, okay?"

"Snacks?" Zeke's face lit up.

"Only one." Akira enveloped them both in a hug, pressing a kiss to the top of his son's head. Then he pulled away and grabbed keys from a jar on a table next to the front door. He flashed Jane a smile. "Five minutes."

* * *

"Melrose Durante. Still using that name, Thoth?" Jean-Claude pronounced the word properly as *towt*. Bringing back memories of the sun. The trickle of water in their courtyard fountain. The coppery scent of blood from cups their mother set before them, freshly bled from the empty-eyed servant that followed her like a whipped dog.

And Jane wondered why Melrose rarely shared stories from his childhood.

He cleared his throat. "Father Girard. Leave."

The priest made for the doors at the back of the church. Jean-Claude flicked his wrist, and they slammed shut. Another flick. The doors at the front swung with even more force, their impact shaking the frames. Girard's face paled and he backed against the wall.

Jean-Claude smirked. "No, I think the good priest should stay. After all, it isn't every day he gets to see a righteous vampire accuse a villainous traitor."

Melrose's pulse jolted. He rolled his shoulders back, letting the action still any fear. The demon inside his brother loved fear. "Still using the occult?"

"I'm using power that works. Unlike you, wasting your time on a God who delights in his children suffering." Jean-Claude turned to the priest. "That is in the Scriptures, right? Something about the death of saints being precious?" His blue eyes hardened. "And they say vampires are bloodthirsty."

God help me. There was no point in arguing with the creature. His brother had given himself over centuries ago. But there was still the matter of the priest, who had moved to a corner, clutching his rosary beads and muttering under his breath. Hopefully something useful, although Melrose would take all the prayer he could get at this point.

"No words? Naturally. There's nothing to argue against. For a man of reason, you've always been terrible at making any case for yourself, Melrose." Jean-Claude sighed. "Perhaps I need to get your attention more."

He was about to twitch his fingers again, but Melrose cut in. "Aren't you four days early, brother?"

"So the tramp *did* deliver my message." Jean-Claude lowered his hands. "I have to say, of all the tarts to waste your time on, a runaway Paxena is lowering even your standards. Her mind snapped after four years. Some of my finest work."

Anger lit his skin on fire. Melrose exhaled slowly, trying to force the burning away. It would only cloud his mind. "The forces that control you never claimed her. So you failed."

"Perhaps. But I left a broken shell. I hope your God finds her sacrifice precious."

Hitting him was stupid. Jean-Claude had centuries of occultism to use. But that didn't stop Melrose from raising his fists.

He'd seen Jean-Claude's torture chambers. Only now, Melrose involuntarily inserted Jane's small frame into each hideous contraption.

Perhaps he'd get in one punch. His arm swung towards Jean-Claude's face.

"Halt." Jean-Claude waved his hand and stopped the blow, holding Melrose's fist in an invisible vise grip.

Pressure crushed his flesh and bones from all sides. Melrose stared at his hand, summoning the power that had first appeared two thousand years ago. Pure light energy seeped out from his pores, pushing away Jean-Claude's dark grip like soap pushed away grime.

The feeling returned to his fingers. He yanked his hand away and flexed the knuckles. Negating dark magic had kept him alive for millennia. But as always, it only cancelled out darkness. It never allowed him to go offensive.

Not that Melrose truly wanted to. Enough blood was spilled already.

"Ah, our usual impasse." Jean-Claude smirked, though his eyes seethed. "Charming. In regards to your question about the timing of my little invasion, do you really think I would tell a slave the truth? I'd rather give you hope—and then rip it away from you."

He gestured. The doors behind him slammed open, allowing the humid night air into the cool cathedral. Melrose turned. A figure in a long trench coat and broad-brimmed hat stood in the doorway.

His heart stuttered.

"Conan."

The figure chuckled and moved aside. Three more stood behind him.

Vampires.

"Melrose Durante, your time has come."

CHAPTER TEN
A CRIMSON BLOSSOM

Melrose dropped to the floor, rolling to the side.

Dark powers, he could neutralize. But bullets sliced through all humans, vampire and Blood Kind included. From the blasts that echoed off the high ceilings and splintered holes in the pews, the shooters had far too much ammunition and an itchy trigger finger.

"A lovely reunion, dear brother. But I'm afraid I must leave you in the hands of my capable assistant." Jean-Claude flashed him a winning smile. "After all, *I* would never kill *my* family." He paused, as if savoring the words. He would. "Besides, I believe Conan has a bone to pick with your surrogate daughter. Such as she is."

"*Bonum est faciet.*" Melrose crawled through the pews, careful not to knock his legs on the kneeler. Bad enough that his skin touched the cold stone floor. How many times would he have to wash his hands? Ten? Twenty?

"Good riddance indeed." An old face greeted him at the end of the aisle. The priest, Girard.

Melrose raised his eyebrows. "That wasn't Church Latin."

Girard shrugged. "I took the vulgate in high school. Quite an

impressive show back there."

Another stream of bullets sprayed the pews. "Regrettably, it doesn't work against projectiles."

"So, we pray." Girard nodded with a weary sigh. "To think, a month ago I performed penance for the sin of boredom."

Melrose smirked and opened his mouth to answer. But another voice echoed first.

"King Melrose Durante, I don't have all night." Conan's voice boomed above him. "I would rather keep my vampires occupied with killing every human in this city."

Only the humans? Quebec City was filled with rehabilitated Blood Kind. Including the Vectorix enforcers. There had to be more to Jean-Claude's plan.

Not a comforting thought.

An ant prickled his skin. Melrose swallowed and flung the

tiny creature away, forcing himself to keep crawling. The priest made a signal, gesturing towards the front altar. Perhaps a hidden door on the side?

Conan's voice continued, "Surrender now, and you will die in peace. Then we'll take the slut princess Zurina and dissect her. Just like we dissected your wife."

A hard, cold weight settled in Melrose's stomach. The words were amateur jibes by an insane man. The truth settled his emotions, lessened the weight. The one thing he couldn't do was lose control. He could never lose control.

God would decide the outcome.

Bullets echoed again.

One way or another.

* * *

The compact car smelled of cheap air freshener and old olive oil. Jane guessed one was meant to cover up the other, but instead the odors swirled together in the breezes flowing in through the open windows. Apparently running houses of mercy didn't pay well. Not enough to pay for air conditioning.

Or for a six-cylinder engine. The little faded orange sedan lurched up and down the hills of Quebec City, rumbling complaints.

Jane kicked the tip of her sneaker against the side of the footwell. Each impatient movement synchronized with the metallic ting of a triangle.

Her grandmother had rows of triangles, made into wind

chimes that clinked along her wide front porch in the Paxena Preserve. Each of them making a slightly different ting-tong tingling sound. Father had always scolded Jane for running along the porch and clanging the cymbals together with her fingers.

Clang-cling-clong-clang!

"Can't we go any faster?" She spoke as much to alleviate the sound as any other reason.

Zuri glanced back, her eyes soft with sympathy. She'd changed into cargo pants, boots, and a long-sleeved purple shirt. "The Vectorix House gives us a lot of sway with the Quebec City police, but not that much. We're nearly there."

It's not enough. Lucy cackled in her head, her acid voice tinged with malice. *We'll be too late, like we always are. Silly spacey-Janey can't ever keep up—*

"Shut up!" Jane slapped her hands over her ears, focusing on the tingling triangles.

She knew the words. The mocking insecurities that haunted her from the Preserve. That drove her to run and find herself in anything else. The Rules of Separation never saved anyone. They only kept Blood Kind from experiencing life.

"Are you all right?"

Jane shrugged. For some reason, the kindness in Zuri's eyes opened her mouth. "I'm Cryptaro. But my family's from Paxena House. Like, all my family. Only I never wanted to be."

"I see." The compassion in Zuri's eyes deepened. She paused, and then asked quietly, "Do they know about you and Uncle Melrose?"

The triangles whipped into a fury of tinkling and clanging. A sharp contrast to the night sky, which had cleared up from the daytime rainstorms and was now filled with a warm haze. "That we're married? No. It wasn't any of their business."

Lucy's sharp voice escaped through her throat. "They wouldn't have cared anyway. They never cared about what I was passionate about, what I wanted."

Jane slapped her hands over her mouth and bit her tongue to avoid further talk. If nothing else, she badly needed to confess. Needed to cleanse herself of the bitterness that Conan and Jean-Claude had inflamed within her.

Zuri reached back and rested a hand on Jane's knee. "I'm sorry."

Akira cleared his throat and began whispering in French. Nothing recognizable this time, but still soothing.

"Thanks." Jane's muscles loosened, and she flopped back against the seat. Tried to distract her mind from the moment. "Why does Vectorix House listen to you?"

Zuri paused, facing forward again. She was silent for so long that Jane wondered if the other woman had heard the words. Finally, she spoke. "I ran away too from a House once. Then, I ran away from a second House. Now, I'm part of Regeleus. Perhaps I'm still running."

Akira placed his hand over hers, squeezing. "*Je t'aime.* We serve God, and that is enough."

"*Dankeshein.*"

German? Vir Vectorix was German. From the pictures, Jane remembered the leader of Vectorix House having hazel eyes very similar to Zuri's. Before Jane could follow up with a question, the car pulled into a parking lot and jerked to a stop. The locks jumped up with a plastic click. Jane twisted the door handle, her feet hitting the pavement and running before Akira or Zuri could stop her. Melrose was inside.

She had to reach him.

Her soles pounded over the sidewalk, up to the front door. She pushed through the heavy wooden panels.

Right into the path of a figure in a dark fedora and trench coat, with brown eyes that widened in shock. Then narrowed, his lips curled into a satisfied smirk as he aimed a pistol at her.

A moment later, her chest exploded in agony and blood.

CHAPTER ELEVEN
The Living and the Dead

Conan didn't favor evil laughs. He left that sort of movie villain nonsense to Jean-Claude.

All the same, a chuckle escaped him at the sight of the woman clutching her chest as she collapsed on the ground, her face twisted into a grimace of pain. About time the scrawny runt did something useful. Even her time as a messenger had failed, at least according to rumors. She didn't execute half the people she was sent after, and never drank live blood.

Unfit for use in their great cause.

"Jane!"

That would be Melrose. Finally, the old man revealed his true weakness, running out of his hiding place near the altar and falling to his knees beside his wife. His back was an easy target.

Conan's finger hovered over the trigger. Jane could still do her damage if the Blood Kind leader died. Finally, one less impediment to Conan's own ascension to power.

Then the planet won't be large enough for you to hide. Melrose must suffer far worse than death.

A shudder rolled through his muscles. He grabbed the pew in front of him. Jean-Claude's voice, as silky as it was deadly. Whether or not the voice was real, the threat certainly was. Conan wasn't strong enough to resist or to defeat the vampire leader.

Not yet.

Jean-Claude's orders were clear. His brother was to suffer as much as possible before death.

More bullets echoed through the church, but not from his men. The Japanese mutt Yamamoto stood at the entrance, his eyes narrowed as he picked off Conan's vampires. Yamamoto. The experiment that never should have happened. Jean-Claude played with fire when he tried to make a multi-strain vampire.

Akira's voice rang out. "Father Girard, leave! We'll contact you later."

So, the priest lived after all. More the pity. But that signaled Conan's own exit. He released his grip on the pew and ducked down, making for a side exit. The dead vampires were collateral. He would have many more at his command soon enough.

The Reclamation would return all Blood Kind to their proper place.

* * *

She would live. She had to.

After all, hadn't she healed from the other injuries? It was entirely possible Jane would heal from these as well.

None of that slowed Melrose's thoughts or caused him to press less firmly against the blood-soaked part of her torso. A pinprick from a needle was far different from a bullet. And he hadn't been able to study or test any aspect of her strange healing ability.

He had been far too busy comforting her. A role he cherished, to be sure, but one that was entirely useless in helping her now. If she had only spoken with him a little, shared any part of her captivity!

Anger heated his veins, but he pushed it down with every pulse of lifeblood from his wife's body. Blood—had the blood slowed?

Footsteps pounded towards him. "Uncle? Who did this?"

"Conan."

Zuri crouched across from him, her face schooled into the businesslike expression he'd encouraged during her childhood. Akira stood sentinel, training a pistol on the door, his eyes searching the area for any physical or spiritual threats.

Melrose cleared his throat. "Anything?"

Akira's brow wrinkled. "Always something. A great conflict, right now, I think. But no vampires nearby."

"Keep me appraised."

"*Oui*. Keep praying."

Prayer? Melrose sighed. At all times, so it went.

Zuri touched his hand. "How severe?"

Back to the moment. "A direct hit just below the ribcage."

"Time since impact?"

"Approximately one and a half minutes." The blood flow had definitely slowed. Melrose's breath hitched. "Emergency first aid?"

"Right here." She opened a first aid kit, her fingers hovering over the contents.

"Sterilization of the-"

Jane spasmed, arching up. Her scars glared red against her pale skin, as if the interior of each mark were wet with fresh blood. A groan escaped her throat, and she clenched her arms over her chest and fell back to the floor. A moment later, the scent of coppery-sweet blood wafted from her body, an intoxicating liquor that called to Melrose's own desires. Desires he hadn't indulged in millennia.

Akira's mouth curled in disgust. Zuri tilted her head to the side, her sweet features puzzled.

"What is that, Uncle?"

Another heart-wrenching cry left Jane's mouth, and her skin began to regain a little more color. The scars flamed even brighter. Melrose rubbed his forehead, heedless of the blood smeared across it.

"No. She's healing." He pushed off the blood-scent, focusing his mind on the present. On lifting his wife into his arms. "We need to return to the house for further examination."

Joy seeped through him, irrational joy, beyond all of the doubts about this situation. Jane was alive. Somehow, that had to be a gift.

The drive home was a distant experience of the rattling engine and the summer breeze that filtered through the windows. A welcome respite from the heat and the scent of blood. All they needed was to get to the house and check her condition. The odor could be a number of issues.

Melrose could solve it. This was mere medicine.

The car halted in front of the three-story Victorian. Akira glanced back at him. "Go in and help her. I'll collect Zeke from the Vectorix station."

Zurina nodded, pressing a kiss to Akira's cheek. "Return quickly, *tomodachi*."

"In God's will, *ma belle*."

She squeezed his hand tightly, then exited the car and opened the side door. Melrose stepped out carefully, cradling Jane close.

Inside the house, they quickly made for the examination room. Zuri began washing her hands as Melrose settled Jane onto the bed.

His goddaughter cleared her throat. "Your turn, Uncle." Jane's body convulsed, every part of her skin flaring with blood vessels. He ran to her side, holding her arms down lest she jolt herself off the bed. "Jane. You're safe. I'm here."

"No one's safe." Her eyes sprang open, bloodshot and wild. "It has begun."

CHAPTER TWELVE
MYTHOLOGY, MURDER, MARRIAGE

"You have to kill me. It's the only way."

Even as Jane spoke the words, she knew they weren't hers. Jean-Claude had spoken them into her ear over and over as he drove more of the dark liquid into her scars. Sealing the command into her psyche, until Lucy had emerged as a way to protect her from the horrific things she'd endured.

But that didn't make them any less true.

Long, languid strains of piano music filled her ears, the minor key of Beethoven's Moonlight Sonata. Jane's stomach squeezed. Jean-Claude had timed his procedures effortlessly to the lingering notes.

Melrose studied her, his face set into that remote mask of thought. "How do you suggest I do that? You healed from a major gunshot wound."

"Yes, but it only-" She ravaged for the word. Closing her eyes, traveling back into the dim room, the leather straps pinning her arms down. Recalling the words spoken around her through the sickening music. "-activated me. Conan shot me on purpose because he knew it wouldn't kill me. It activated the latent virus."

Behind Melrose, Zuri stiffened. She backed up to the corner sink and cabinets, the latex gloves in her hand, her eyes dark with concern and fear. At least one of the two had some sense.

Melrose only frowned. "What sort of virus?"

The sonata grew louder in her head, distancing Jean-Claude's voice and the memories. Bile rose in her throat. "I don't know."

"Jane, if you could only clear your mind and focus-"

"I don't know!" She slammed her fists onto the edges of the table. "I was strapped to a bed—and his fingers were on my skin, and—"

Jane bent her knees up and pulled them close beneath her chin. Any courage she'd had vanished in the onslaught. All the pain and the music and the constant reminder that she was a monster. No one had been there to save her. Only the prayers she whispered in the darkness of her mind while Lucy took over.

Out of the corner of her eye, she saw Melrose turn away, his jaw working. Maybe that was the way things ended after all. What use could she possibly be to him? She wasn't even strong enough to face her memories.

God, I'm sorry. I don't want to be here anymore.

"Just kill me. Before I do anything worse."

A long pause. For a moment, Melrose's expression didn't change. "Zurina, please leave the room."

She nodded. "I'll check on the security systems."

The door closed silently behind her. Everything was consumed by the quiet, inevitable sound of the sonata, caressing her mind the way Jean-Claude lovingly caressed her scars.

My perfect weapon.

Jane stared down at her knees. Tears burned at the corners of her eyes. A scudding of metal over linoleum, and the nearness of breath. A warm brown hand tilted her chin up, until she stared into Melrose's eyes, filled with naked pain.

"I'm not going to kill you."

"You have to. Jean-Claude said that's the only way."

He shook his head. "My brother is a consummate liar."

"Then have someone else do it. I know you abide by 'first, do no harm,' but you can just find someone else. You're the king of the Blood Kind."

Melrose's fingers gently traced her cheek, up to her ear. Softening the inner music with his touch. "Do you know why I made that vow?"

She shrugged. "Because you're a physician?"

His fingers stopped, and he pulled away a little. Like he always did. The sadness grew in his face. "Because killing my family nearly destroyed me."

* * *

"So you are a murderer."

Jane shifted back on the bed, her green eyes harsh and fearful. Naturally, they were. That was why he had pulled back first. Far easier to make the first move.

"My parents were part of an ancient Egyptian cult of vampires. At first, many were priests of Anubis, embalmers, which gave them access to the blood drained during the mummification process."

His wife wrinkled her nose. "So you were a priest?"

Melrose sighed, steepling his fingers. "Of a sort. I was raised in that environment, and I had a gift for the work. As the first-born, I was expected to go into service and so ensure that my parents and family would have access to blood. Then I realized the peculiar nature of vampire embalming."

He paused. "I warn you, this isn't pleasant."

"The last five years weren't pleasant. This is honesty." Jane still watched him warily. "Go on."

"Under the guise of Anubis priests, the vampires drugged people in such a way as to mimic death and then carried on various rituals of drinking their blood directly from the source. My parents were exceptionally clever, and developed complicated methods of extraction to enhance the experience and honor the gods—or themselves. I could never discern which. But I couldn't endure it. At my first observation of the ritual, when I was fifteen, I ran away, stealing a pouch of gold to pay for travel. Something within me abhorred every part of the cult. Divine conviction, I suppose." He rubbed his forehead. "After some years of misad-venture and feeding on animal blood, which as we know isn't adequate, I entered the Lyceum, founded by Aristotle. The logic and reason there were comforting, and seemed to fill the void in my mind. I remained in Greece for hundreds of years. The only contact I had with my family was with my brother, Ramos. Jean-Claude. At that point, he had taken up with our sister."

"Gross," Jane muttered.

"It was considered entirely acceptable." Melrose's lips twitched. "But I agree. By then, I had developed a sufficiently advanced method of blood transfusion. I hoped it would replace the blood drinking. Perhaps, at least, I could reclaim my brother and sister from the cult and introduce them to reason. When I wrote of it to Jean-Claude, he seemed receptive."

She leaned forward on the metal examination table, dangling her legs off the edge. Likely in mere interest. Jane was always drawn into his stories. "But you said he was a consummate liar."

The words sank inside him. "A habit he apparently learned early. My family had relocated to Alexandria by that point in time. I stayed there for a while, in separate quarters, attempting to reason with them. Nothing was effective. And then—"

The room faded as the memories took hold. Shouts from the distance. Melrose raced out to his balcony, sighting the army across the flat tops of buildings and narrow patches of cultivated gardens. Over 20,000 soldiers, armed and arrayed in full battle gear. His lips parted, hot air drying his throat. Caesar's forces couldn't withstand the attack. His family must flee.

Melrose was off. Running down the stone steps of his small apartment, across the narrow streets to the center of the Egyptian part of the city. Throwing open the door to his family's quarters, only to learn that they were utterly unconcerned. Pothinus, the scheming eunuch behind the throne of Ptolemy, was a vampire. He had orchestrated the whole conflict between the Egyptian heirs Cleopatra and Ptolemy, even though it turned against him. The upcoming battle, while terrible for many, would provide a wealth of dying for vampires to feast upon. Melrose's parents and siblings were well prepared to harvest.

"It was then that I realized they had to be stopped. Their actions before were despicable enough, but these secret machinations and massacres could not be allowed to continue. There was far too much potential for escalation. During the battle, I named my family as traitors and enemies of Rome. Roman forces were desperate to release their vengeance. It was far too easy to arrange."

"So you didn't actually kill them yourself?"

Jane's voice cut through the harsh images from the past. The arid climate of Egypt was replaced by the harsh smell of disinfectant. Melrose released his shoulders, rolling them back. "Not physically. Except for one."

Remembering Aneksi's face, the agony in her eyes. He'd barely known her, as she had been born a century after he'd left. And yet, her expression, the blood trickling down her head, still pierced his mind. "My sister tried to escape, killing anyone in her path. I never knew she could wield such dark powers. I had shunned all of that. Yet, I had always been a good shot with a spear."

Jane chewed on her lower lip. "I have a sister. Thirty years younger. Paula."

"I am glad."

She paused. "So, after that?"

"It is as I told you before. I returned to Greece. While there, missionaries from a strange sect of Judaism passed through. Their main speaker was eloquent. And loud. But he managed to reason effectively with the great scholars. And so, I converted."

"I still can't believe you heard St. Paul—or that you thought he was obnoxious."

"But intelligent." Melrose paused. But the words had to be said. "Jane, the reason you are a target is due to your marriage to me. Jean-Claude wants to hurt me, as often and as terribly as he can. It's been his mission ever since he escaped. If you hadn't married me, you would have escaped his notice entirely. But I was selfish. I thought I could keep you safe."

She reached out, and he flinched at her touch on his fingers. But Jane only held tighter. She slipped off the table and nudged her way into his lap, wrapping her arms around him. "I'm sorry."

"For what?" A part of him blared warning signals at Jane's proximity, for the virus she supposedly carried. But that part was silenced by the relief that she was still there.

Even after knowing the truth.

"For doubting you. For not seeing how much you needed support. I had no idea."

He stared up into her eyes. "I never knew I needed it, until I met you."

Jane grinned a little, her cheeks flushing. Entirely beautiful. He ran his fingers through her cropped hair, tracing the line of her neck. She leaned into his touch with a soft exhale.

The door burst open.

"Uncle!" Zuri clutched a cell phone in one hand and the security system remote with the other. "It's the police station. The Vectorix are attacking."

He sat up, and Jane placed her feet back on the floor. Her

hands still clutched his arms. "Attacking who?"

"Every healthy human. And it's not just them. All the Blood Kind in the city are acting-"

Suddenly, it clicked in Melrose's mind. "-like vampires."

CHAPTER THIRTEEN
DANGER MAKES THE BLOOD FLOW

Zuri pointed the cell phone at Melrose like a weapon. "Yes, they're all acting like vampires. How do you know that?"

A gong sounded in Jane's mind. She snorted. In other circumstances, it would have been funny. But right now, all she cared about was dealing with this virus inside her, one way or another.

Death was no longer the answer. She'd seen how selfish that was, how much it would hurt Melrose. All this time, she had thought she was staying out of his way and giving him freedom, while preserving her own independence. It was only weakening both of them.

Basically, she was an idiot. It was time to deal with that.

Jane turned to Melrose. "When I almost died and came back to life, was there any weird smell? Taste?"

"Blood. It reminded me of the last burst of blood-life before death, but it only grew stronger." He paused. "Irresistible, nearly, although I'm well experienced in resisting the taste, and some are entirely immune."

He glanced at Zuri.

His goddaughter's face pinched. "Akira and Zeke are trapped in the Vectorix station. He says the Vectorix are acting mad. He and Zeke are in one of the maximum security cells for now."

An image flashed in her mind of the good-natured man and child, huddled in a corner while ravenous vampires—armed with their own incredible strength as well as actual weapons—tried to force them out. Even the reinforced walls wouldn't last forever. Another low reverberating thrum, like a musical vacuum cleaner.

Jane closed her eyes, forcing her mind back through the memories. Pushing herself to recall every excruciating detail. "When you drove back here, were the windows down?"

"Yes. Akira said he could barely focus because of the scent."

The cool night breezes, whipping across her skin and blowing the scent out into Quebec City. Her heart sank. "Then the damage has been done. I'm sorry."

Zuri glared at her. "What damage?"

"Jean-Claude didn't just want to torture you by forcing you to kill me." Jane glanced at Melrose. "The words he brainwashed into me were true. This city will be overrun by vampires. By turning the Blood Kind into them."

Her husband leaned forward, his chin perched on his fingers. "That's impossible. Vampirism is a choice to drink the blood of humans. The act of drinking produces the chemical addiction."

Jane gestured to the scars on her arms. "Yes, but what if he found a way to make the chemical triggers of blood-drinking airborne? Any Blood Kind who breathed in that air would be activated."

"They could resist the compulsion. I did."

Sometimes the man's arrogance was ridiculous. "Not everyone is as strong as you, Melrose. If they had no faith, no purpose, nothing to anchor them against the addiction except the Blood Kind laws? If they were Vectorix, who are already hypersensitive?"

His face tightened. "Zuri, you need to go to the station. Get Akira and Zeke out of there. Kill if you must."

Zuri hesitated. "Those are Vectorix."

Melrose stood and placed his hands on her shoulders, his expression softening. "At this point, they are vampires. I won't have you losing your family too. Get them out."

Her shoulders straightened, then she raced out of the room.

Another heavy tone. This time, the gong held a metallic crash.

Jane raised her eyebrows and turned to Melrose. "So, what's our plan? Take out all of the infected Blood Kind in the city?"

* * *

If it came to that.

Melrose didn't voice the words, but the edge in Jane's voice signaled he didn't need to. And that she would fight him all the way for another solution.

Another reason he was glad she was there.

"I was considering ways of containing them." He grimaced. "Although since this is an airborne virus, I doubt we'll have much hope of that."

"Killjoy."

"What would you suggest?" Melrose walked over to the prep sink and washed his hands. Settling into the comforting rhythm of soap and friction. Rinsing. Repeating, taking care to get every crevice.

The scent of blood suffused him as she drew near and rested a hand on his forehead. "What's this? The dried blood?"

"Yours." He sluiced more of the soap off his hands. "From when I applied pressure to the bullet wound."

"You never washed it off?"

"I'd forgotten about it."

She shook her head. "You'll scrub your hands raw. Because that makes sense."

"Absolutely."

Jane grabbed a handful of paper towels and shoved them under the running water. She swiped at his forehead, spattering droplets of water in his eyes. "What if you made an antidote? Stopped me from being contagious and then released something to cancel out the spread."

"I already considered that idea. And abandoned it." Melrose's skin burned from her efforts. He winced. He needed to get better quality paper towels. But it wasn't worth pushing away his wife. Not when she was finally reaching out, in some small way. "I would need precise measurements and details of what was done to you to even begin."

"What if I could give you crystal clear knowledge of everything?"

Enough. There couldn't possibly be any blood left on his face. He caught her hand in his and gently squeezed it. "Every time you try to remember, it destroys you."

"This is more important than the pain. Or the fear." She squeezed back. "You need my help."

Wonder spread through him. Was this what it felt like to have someone supporting you?

A series of loud bangs jolted him out of the thoughts.

Jane gripped his hands more tightly. "What was that?"

A chill crept up his spine. "The external security system."

"And that means?"

"Steel barriers over every door and window." He pulled his wife close. "In case vampires attack the house."

She tilted her chin up. "Then let's start."

BLOOD MERCY

CHAPTER FOURTEEN
SURFACING FROM THE DEPTHS

Moonlight Sonata lilted through her memories, its minor key luring her back into captivity. Only this time she wasn't alone, clinging desperately to the promises of release from pain and trying to stave off the worst of the vampire influence.

She prayed. She focused. And she sat on the examination table next to Melrose. Who wasn't leaving. Who never stopped fighting the darkness, even when it cost him his own family. She heard a vinyl squeak as he shifted on the folding chair. Then clicking as his fingers entered information into his laptop. "What do you see?"

Jane slipped through the memory, focusing on visuals. She'd closed her eyes the majority of the time, but she'd caught a few glimpses of vials on a table next to the bed. "Sodium chloride solution, dextrose-"

"Those are for the IV. Can you see anything more unusual?"

She sighed. "Not really. As I mentioned, he had me strapped to a bed."

A pause. "Did he ever-"

She pressed her lips together. "Not that I remember. He never failed to tell me what a useful slave I was, or how despicable I was. Often in the same sentence." Time for another search. "I'm going to try listening again. Although it's hard to hear through the music."

"In your mind?"

"No. In the memory. Apparently he's a fan of Beethoven. Hang on, I'm getting something. He's talking into a voice recorder. Making notes, I think. Gamma-aminobutyric acid?"

"An inhibitory neurotransmitter that can be involved with addiction. Keep listening."

She pushed through the piano, through the waves of pain that always accompanied the memories. Seeking out the words. These were her memories. This was her mind, and she had survived for a reason: to help others escape.

She didn't have to be a weapon. She could heal.

"Okay, I hear more." Jane listed off ingredients. Methods. Random comments using long, complicated chemical names that might as well have been in another language. "-and he just said 'prefrontal cortex' again."

An explosion boomed through the house. The medical supplies rattled on the shelves. Flakes of paint fell from the ceiling. Jane's eyes flew open. Melrose still hunched over his laptop, the screen filled with complicated spreadsheets and charts. "What was that?"

"Some kind of effort to get inside the house, I would think. Considering his response, I would say it was probably Conan.

Jean-Claude never dirties his fingers with mundane takeovers."

He picked at the collar of his shirt, fidgeting with the edge. Leaving it popped up. Jane resisted the urge to fix it. "How can you talk about it so calmly?"

"Previous experience." Did he just wink at her? A faint smile curved his generous lips. Lips that suddenly seemed very appealing, if she didn't want to smack him for being so dang calm. "Please, try to center yourself and continue. I think I've narrowed down the possibilities to a few solutions."

She closed her eyes and descended into the memories again. Bracing herself as the pain seized her muscles. This was a different scene. A lot closer to the present.

When I emerged.

Lucy. The bitterness curled around Jane's mind. Her fingers clutched the edge of the medical table.

"You are me," she whispered. "And I'm not scared anymore."

You will be. For a moment, the strains of the sonata surrounded her in thick, suffocating ribbons of sound, blocking out thought, much less any sense of reality. *Do you really think he will save you? You need me. You need to protect yourself.*

She felt Melrose's hands on hers. "Jane? I'm here. Please, stay strong. We can do this."

He's lying. He doesn't trust you and he never will.

"Shut up. He's not lying. You are." She sighed and opened her eyes. "I am."

Her husband tilted his head to the side, studying her with compassion and an edge of impatience. But that was fair. She'd never really committed to anything in this relationship. Never tried to be there for him, except when it was fun and she felt in the mood.

Even when she knew he needed help.

"I'm sorry." Jane swallowed. "I'm sorry for pretending I didn't see your issues. I'm sorry for ignoring all of your serious conversations about the Houses. I'm sorry for acting like this relationship was a vacation. I guess I was intimidated by who you are. What you've done. And I couldn't imagine why you'd want me around for as long as we can live, so I assumed it wouldn't last."

Melrose's eyes crinkled with deep hurt. "I meant those vows. I never stopped looking for you. I should have been more open about it, but I was scared that if Jean-Claude knew I searched for you, he would kill you to hurt me further. I couldn't endanger you. I'm sorry that you felt abandoned."

"I forgive you."

The sonata fell silent.

A shudder escaped her, punctuated by another explosion that rocked the foundations of the house.

Followed by a furious pounding at the door. It whammed open.

"Uncle! They've breached the walls."

*   *   *

Zuri's hair lay wild and tangled on her shoulders, her eyes bright with desperation. Blood streaked her clothing, which was scratched and ripped in parts. She clutched a pistol in one hand

and a knife in the other.

The Vectorix warrior she'd never wanted to be. But it had always lurked beneath the surface, along with her mysterious gifts.

Melrose pressed a kiss to Jane's lips, saw the understanding in her face. He turned to Zuri. "Did you make it to the station?"

She shook her head. "They ambushed me when I stepped off the front porch. I tried to hold the upstairs, but there were too many. Conan. This is personal."

"Naturally." Melrose held her gaze, keeping his tone level. Letting her draw strength from his calm. "How long until they get down here?"

"An hour. Maybe less." Zuri glanced at Jane. "Did you come to a solution?"

Melrose followed her gaze and nodded at his wife. Urging her to speak for herself, instead of hiding around others as she preferred. This was her fight too. She was the queen of the Blood Kind.

With all the difficulties and hard decisions that entailed.

Jane cleared her throat, wiping her palms on her pant legs. "I managed to recall most of what Jean-Claude mentioned about the virus. I might be able to figure out a little more."

She closed her eyes, her shoulders slumping as she turned inward. Easier and quicker than before. Melrose's heart swelled with pride. Thank God. She'd broken free.

"The addictive serum was fed into my body over the years through the scars. They're the release gateway to the contagion. The virus is actually a stimulant, laced with a chemical compound that infected my sweat glands, enabling the chemicals to coat my skin. All that's necessary to disperse them is wind."

"Thank you." Melrose typed furiously at his keyboard. Adjusting one formula, running new algorithms for possible chemical compounds. "Jean-Claude is creative, but he is also lazy. He tends to use the same formulas in all of his work. I might be able to synthesize something in the laboratory and at least coat your skin with it to neutralize the virus. Later I can treat the deeper conditions, but that should be sufficient for now."

Jane tapped the edge of the table. "But what about dispersal? We'd have to get it around all of Quebec City. I can't control the wind."

"No. *You* can't." Melrose studied Zuri.

Her face paled. "You can't expect—I can't, not without—"

"Without what?" Jane blinked.

Zuri set her jaw. "Uncle, I haven't tried in decades."

He stood, never breaking eye contact. "Then I would pray that you relearn quickly, Zurina. For all our sakes."

CHAPTER FIFTEEN
HIDING AND KILLING THE PAST

At last, they were caught in their own precious hovel. Like rats in a hole.

"Destroy everything."

Conan swaggered through the front rooms, picking up and knocking off all objects that rested on a table or shelf. Never before had he been able to do so. Mistress Zurina had been far too good at covering her tracks and holding lightly to material possessions. She and her husband both.

But there, in Quebec City, she had grown soft. Relaxed her guard and allowed herself to acquire trinkets. Books with inscriptions and signatures. Photos featuring gatherings and events with friends. Conan waved a hand, summoning a slave. He never bothered learning the names. All of the trench-coated underlings looked the same.

"Find each of them and drain them. Enjoy it. Keep the corpses. I'm certain our master will want the princess to view their state."

The woman nodded. "Is there anything else?"

"Yes. Dispatch additional forces to the Vectorix station to

ensure they are receiving the full dose."

"Yes."

She turned to leave. Conan snapped his fingers and turned his index finger once, stirring the slightest bit of magic combined with mesmerism. With the small gesture, the slave turned around. "Do you forget yourself?"

"Yes. Sir. It would be my honor to serve."

"Far better."

Although Jean-Claude's dark magic tricks were quite annoying at times, they were, on occasion, very convenient. Conan was the chief lieutenant of the vampire master. Moreover, he was a Talamar prince by blood and birthright.

No one would steal that from him again.

He spied another picture on the shelf, of Mistress Zurina with a baby in her arms. A rare Blood Kind child. As rare as his own child had been—should have been—if Aleron hadn't stolen the beautiful Karina from him and taken her virtue. Taken the dearest prize Conan had won.

Aleron, always Mistress Zurina's favorite among the two of them. Aleron, the favorite of Gabrel Talamar. The selfish brat was protected by both of them.

When the Vectorix harpy was captured, the others would fall. Conan had amended his view of her life. Jean-Claude could do all he wanted to extract her power. The greater the danger to Mistress Zurina, the greater the likelihood Gabrel would expose himself to save her, no matter how sordid and dramatic their break-up.

The Talamar leader yet had his weaknesses.

Conan lifted the picture frame and slipped the photo from it. This, he would keep, and show to Mistress Zurina when chains bound her.

A worthy reminder of all she had lost.

"Lord Conan! We've nearly breached the door to the basement."

A smile curved his lips. Mistress Zurina had to be delivered alive. Jean-Claude had never specified unharmed.

"Not a moment too soon."

* * *

Jane opened her mouth. Closed it before she asked Melrose again if the serum was ready.

She'd already asked him five times during his work. The lines in his forehead as he moved the serum from one spinning apparatus to another chemical-testing apparatus made it clear he didn't need to be disturbed. Thousands of years of life gave him a lot of patience, but she wasn't interested in testing limits.

Not with the sonata finally replaced with a gentle, melodic humming. The lullabies Jane's mother had murmured over her as she went to sleep. Far more comforting, although the songs brought a pang of guilt. When this was all over, she needed to contact the Preserve and fill them in on the details. Before, she thought they'd make her stay, but now that she was technically the queen of the Blood Kind, that wasn't really a concern.

Jane did another survey of the small laboratory, a square room identical to the examination room, but lined with tables and a sink in the corner. She poked at the test tubes, ran her thumb along the edges of the beakers. Twirled the micro-pipette in her fingers. It would be really handy for detailed work—or maybe a henna tattoo design?

Jane set it down and moved along the table to the scale, reaching out to press her palm onto the surface.

"I wouldn't." Zuri's voice, soft and clear. How had she moved from the door so fast? Then again, from Melrose's cryptic request, the woman was capable of many things.

Jane drew her hand back. "Why not?"

"He'll have to recalibrate it. And I think he has enough to worry about without that small nuisance. The small ones annoy him the most."

She smiled, giving Melrose a knowing look. The first expression Jane had seen on her face, other than morose contemplation or frantic swipes at her cell phone. Zuri pulled out the device again, moving quickly through the menus.

Jane nodded towards the phone. "Still no word from Akira?"

"There has to be a good reason. There always is." Zuri slipped the phone back into her pocket, worry flickering over her face.

"Yeah. I mean, you and he have been at this whole taking down bad guys business for a long time, right?"

Zuri nodded, her tan face cautious. But still more open than it had been since they'd moved to the lab. Might be worth a follow-up question. Melrose saw Zuri as his daughter. That meant getting along with her would be especially important.

"Did you meet him in France, then?"

A gentle fondness came over her face. "Yes. I was in Paris in the 1920s, working as a seamstress. My godson was attending classes for priesthood, and he visited when he could, but I was lonely, so I'd go to cafes on some nights. One night, I stopped by the cafe where Akira worked. I enjoyed his cooking, and as I kept returning he found reasons to speak with me, sometimes for hours into the night. Occasionally, he got into trouble for not completing his chores."

"Aw, that's cute. Well, except for him getting into trouble. So you fell in love just like that?"

"Not quite." Zuri gave her a searching look, then continued. "I don't know what Melrose has told you about me. I am of Vectorix House, and that gives me certain privileges and responsibilities. After I left the cafe, I would sometimes patrol the streets. Akira did the same thing. Vampires liked to prey on the tourists and free spirits in 1920s Paris. He has always had trouble sleeping, because of the effects of the experimentation."

An explosion rocked the room above them. Jane pressed against the wall.

Zuri continued quietly. "One night, I was faced with more assailants than I realized. A trap. Akira ran into the fight alongside me." She shook her head ruefully. "He fought so well, I never would have guessed how much it cost him. Afterwards, I took him to my suite and cared for his wounds. He needed so much blood. There, he told me about his past, and he learned mine. Shortly after, we married."

Jane grinned. "How shortly?"

"Three days."

"I'll bet Melrose loved that."

"Oh, he was very perturbed." Zuri chuckled. "He arrived within two days to thoroughly discuss the matter. And Aleron, he-"

"Aleron? As in, Aleron Talamar? Of the London Talamar massacre?"

"Yes."

"You know Aleron Talamar? The brother of that psycho Conan?"

A steel wall covered Zuri's face. She played with the edge of her knife handle. "The Talamars' secrets are their own."

"Yeah. I've heard that." In fact, that was the exact phrase all Talamar House Blood Kind used as a cop-out when refusing to talk about matters. But it had slipped off Zuri's tongue so fluidly.

The wall still covered Zuri's emotions. Whatever the reason for her Talamar connection, Jane wouldn't get it out of the woman now. Perhaps one final question. "So, where were you before Paris?"

"I worked as a governess." Zuri glanced at Melrose. "I believe he is nearly ready."

"Then you'll find a way to disperse the antidote?"

Zuri sighed, tugging at the ends of her loose hair. "It appears we have no other solutions."

CHAPTER SIXTEEN
A LAST BREATH OF WIND

For once, Melrose would have appreciated touching his wife's skin in a non-medical way.

He carefully swabbed the serum on the last of her scars. She had taken off the hooded jacket, leaving her shoulders and arms exposed in her form-fitting tank top. Her pants had been cuffed up to the knee. Even with just those scars coated, the blood scent had greatly lessened. Later, he would take care of the rest.

Her current attire made the prospect of healing her body even more desirable. And it was a far better thing to focus on than the immediate future.

"Hey, Durante. If you're interested, my butt's a little further down." Jane tossed her head, a few strands flipping into her eyes. She glared at the grayish-brown hair. "First thing, I'm growing this out and dyeing it—hm, what color?"

Melrose pushed the hair out of her eyes. "Violet, perhaps?"

"I like that. Maybe with some dark brown undertones. After all, I wouldn't want to scandalize the Blood Kind too much. Since I'm supposed to be a queen and all." The sparkle faded a little from her green eyes, replaced by worry. "What if they don't like me? The Blood Kind. You go to all sorts of events and you meet with world leaders and-"

He placed a finger over her lips. "I wouldn't have married you if I didn't think you were equal to the task. I'll be with you every step of the way."

Her frown deepened. "I wish you could come with me now."

"So do I." He leaned down, brushing her lips with his. "I love you."

A blast shuddered through the building, with an aftermath of creaking, smashing steel. They parted reluctantly.

Jane raised her eyebrows. "So, being attacked. That happens a lot when you're king?"

"With family like mine?"

She cradled his chin in her hands, giving him a sad, knowing smile. Finally understanding a small portion of the grief he carried. They would have a lot more to share.

But for now, they needed to survive.

Jane slipped out of his arms. "Zuri? It's show time."

His goddaughter looked up from her phone, her tight expression revealing no contact from Akira. "Very well."

Melrose glanced at Jane.

She nodded. "So I'll go and inspect the test tubes again. Because there are a lot of them."

"Indeed."

He walked over to Zuri. She stuck the phone in her pocket. "Uncle, I have no idea if this is going to work."

"If it's meant to, it will. You need to believe that, Zurina." He rested his hands on her shoulders.

She rolled her eyes. "Considering what happened last time? I doubt I'm even deserving, Uncle. After what happened with Gabrel?"

"None of us are deserving. If there was ever a time to try, it would be now." He lowered his voice. "Things are growing worse."

Zuri looked away. "So you've said."

"So I mean." He nudged her chin so that she faced him once more. "You have been given gifts for a reason. That reason is not to hide in Regeleus House forever. The Blood Kind need you."

"We'll see." Another crash echoed down the hall. "That's my cue."

He squeezed her shoulders, then released her. "Indeed."

Melrose walked over to the table and grabbed a canister about the size of a can of soda, handing it to Jane along with a scalpel. "This is filled with additional serum, in a gaseous state. Release it as well, and Quebec City should be covered."

Zuri exhaled slowly, her face centering into a mask of concentration.

"I hope so."

*   *   *

Zuri stood in the middle of the hallway, still as a statue. Watching as the steel door twisted off its frame.

"Zuri?" Jane tugged her arm. "Call me crazy, but I don't think this is great for our health. Or future existence."

The Vectorix woman didn't move. Didn't even blink. Her hands remained raised in front of her, palms up, fingers splayed. Her eyes closed.

Worry weighed on Jane's chest. Her mind echoed with the distant sound of pan pipes, from some movie she'd watched a while ago. If she remembered correctly, it had been on the soundtrack as the two armies faced off on a misty morning, marching over a plain.

They were screwed.

"Are you okay? Maybe, if you're not sure, we could escape through another way. I'm sure you have other secret passages or something in this old house, right?"

A last sickening shriek, and the metal door skidded down the stairs, headed right for them. Jane flinched, running back a few steps.

Zuri didn't move, even as the door hit the ground right in front of her feet. Was this some kind of test? Meditation?

Conan moved down the steps. Hat slouched over his brown eyes, aristocratically handsome face drawn into a perpetual sneer. Duster sweeping around him. "Zurina Vectorix. Or should I say, dear Mistress Zurina?"

Her eyes narrowed. "Conan."

"You make this far too easy. Then again, you always did coddle your students, when you weren't neglecting them for your own pleasure. We both know the real reason you were my governess."

Curiosity sparked in Jane's mind, although dampened by the pistol he had pointed at Zuri's head. Still, Zuri didn't move.

The panpipes trilled a piercing scale.

"This time, I won't bother with pretensions. Accidents happen. Even Jean-Claude can understand that."

He pulled the trigger. Zuri's hands thrust out, palms out straight. The walls and stairs shook under the onslaught of wind ripping at the posts and steps. Conan crashed back into the upper stairwell. Zuri twitched her fingers. Another gale-force blast lifted the vampire up and hurtled him through the doorway.

"This way."

Jane's legs were glued to the floor. She was unable to process the human tornado she'd just seen. "Zuri? The stairs, are they safe?"

"Yes, if you walk quickly." She placed one foot in front of the other, the wall of wind surging ahead of her. Jane gulped and followed, trying to stay close behind and out of the side currents that tore at her clothing.

Up the stairs. Through the foyer, the house in shambles around them, a combination of the vampires' destruction and the mini-cyclone Zuri was stirring up. Jane spared a glance around. Akira's kitchen had been ruined, every appliance twisted and broken, the central island smashed in half. The living room on the other side of the entrance was a mess of ripped upholstery and shattered technology.

Anything that was partly whole suffered the destruction of Zuri's winds. Including the vampires who cowered in the corners. She studied them through narrowed eyes, then effortlessly moved the remains of furniture over their hideaways, trapping them in place. Any who resisted, who raised their weapon, she pinned with a concentrated bolt of wind that knocked them unconscious.

So this was what Melrose meant by unique. Special. Jane could buy it, as well as why he'd kept it a secret. She'd heard of the rare Blood Kind who had powers, some kind of special response to the occult forces of darkness.

But this was unreal.

Zuri walked slowly down the front steps, twisting the wind around her. The trees shook along the sidewalk, bending in half, their leaves fluttering frantically. Trash scattered from overturned cans.

She stopped in the middle of the street, turning to face Jane. "Release the canister, then take my hands!"

"Where's Conan?"

"He likely ran away. He's skilled at that." Her mouth twisted in derision. "We have bigger problems. Take my hands before this situation gets any worse!"

"Got it!"

Jane punctured the canister with the scalpel, releasing the antidote gas. Dropped it at their feet. Then grabbed Zuri's hands. "What, are you going to pulverize the city with healing?"

"Something like that!" Her eyes glinted with a fierceness that Jane had never seen, yet her grip was strong and controlled. "Hold on!"

The winds blew faster and faster, surrounding them in a vortex of elemental power. Swirling up into the sky in a narrow column of intensity Jane could almost see.

For once, her mind was silent. Free of the hallucinations. Free of everything but the potent energy sucking at every pore in her skin, siphoning every particle of the antidote.

"One. More. Second." Zuri's eyes shut and her dark hair blown back from her face. "Now!"

She released Jane's hands and flung her arms out to either side. Rising into the air, sending the column pulsing into the sky and out in all directions, blanketing Quebec City in warm gusts. Zuri's arms moved in graceful arcs, guiding the breezes, her lips muttering silent words, eyes still closed.

Dancing with the wind as with an invisible partner. For a moment, a pool of moonlight seemed to surround her.

Zuri's arms fell to her sides. She descended on a soft breeze. Her face turned away from the light, wet with tears.

"Mom?" Zeke's voice trembled.

Jane turned to see the kid, his mouth open in shock, holding the hand of a bloodied, bruised figure with a thatch of dark hair and a weary face.

Akira.

"Zeke?" Zuri began running. Reaching them in a last burst of wind that nearly carried her off the ground. "Akira!"

She flung her arms around him.

Je t'aime. Her husband managed a bright smile.

Then a shadow swallowed the light in his eyes and he collapsed in Zuri's arms.

Motionless.

CHAPTER SEVENTEEN
A WASTELAND OF LILIES

Zuri's hand rested on the casket, her fingers pressing against the smooth, polished ebony. Unlike the rest in the secluded glade, she didn't wear black.

Instead, she wore a dark, charcoal gray skirt and vest over a pale shirt. Zeke was similarly dressed in gray dress pants and pale shirt, his dark head barely visible above the tall grass that choked the abandoned cemetery.

Melrose remembered her aversion to gray as a child. Her assertion that it was far more the color of death. An argument he had difficulty disputing, considering the state of the body after rigor mortis set in.

A fist squeezed his chest.

He'd never wanted Zuri to see that color in the face of her husband. Not after death had taken her mother, and her father had distanced himself in grief.

Not after the London massacre.

Aleron passed his hand over the casket in the traditional movements as he intoned in Latin. His face drawn tightly, a

stark contrast to Zurina's serenity. Her expression was thoughtful and smooth. The mask she wore to bury her sorrow, until she could release it later in private.

There had been a time when he was privy to that, when she would have climbed into his lap and buried her face in his chest, her brown hair curtaining over her face. Now, everyone was shut out, save perhaps for Zeke, who held her hand tightly, his round cheeks streaked with quiet tears.

Jane shifted next to Melrose. She wore the same resignation that hovered over the proceedings like a dark cloud. The hopelessness of those who knew they could be next, no matter how many transfusions they took.

Healthy humans envied the Blood Kind their longevity, their remarkable abilities. They seldom remembered that transfusions could fail, that donated blood be rejected. Death didn't wait for the Blood Kind and gave them no security in when it would strike. A reason Aleron and his cemetery hermitage were always open to offer free burial for the lost. One of the many ways the priest offered penance for his own past, a past that bound him in isolation, even from his godmother.

Jane cleared her throat. "What will Zuri do now?"

"I don't know." He shook his head, watching as the coffin was lowered into the ground by individuals from Vectorix House. Vir Vectorix's one outreach for the son-in-law he barely knew, save for a handful of brief visits.

He should have been here to at least observe the burial of an honorable man. A man who had protected Zeke, Vir's only grandson, from the poisoned Vectorix who were meant to ensure Blood Kind safety. Akira had given far too much, used far too much of his abilities in the process. His overtaxed body had surrendered before it could receive a transfusion. Perhaps Vir and Zuri could have shared in the grief, at last having the cold comfort of common ground. The death of a spouse.

But as always, his friend had been silent when Melrose spoke with him. Leaving Melrose to stand by Zuri.

As he always would.

"...and to dust we return." Aleron finished, closing the Bible.

Melrose walked closer, his wingtips crunching through the grass and debris underfoot. The cracked pieces of stone from the nearby buildings. Jane followed, her gaze distracted by the ancient stonework. Finding rest in the past when the present became unbearable. That, at least, he knew about her.

A vein of dark irony, considering their marriage.

He walked around the grave and paused, watching as Zuri dropped a single white lily into the hole. The flowers she had carried at her wedding. Next to her, Zeke threw in his flower, more tears flowing down his cheeks. They forewent any symbolic gestures involving the mourners throwing dirt into the grave.

How like his goddaughter, to consider Melrose's inconvenient ticks, even then.

Zuri knelt to lift her son into her arms. Aleron placed a hand on her arm and gestured to Melrose. She shifted Zeke into the priest's arms instead. Gently kissed her son's head, then tenderly grasped Aleron's hand in thanks.

At last, she turned to him. Only then did his goddaughter's lips tremble, and her placid expression twisted into grief and tears as she fell into his arms. He held her close, hand on the back of her neck, rubbing the skin there. As he always had when she was younger. Zuri shook in his arms, ready to break like the cracked walls and pillars in the cemetery.

"Shhhh." No words came to his mind through the sorrow. At that moment, only Jane's hand on his back gave Melrose the strength to remain standing.

He knew she prayed. That helped as well.

At last, Zuri lifted her head, her hazel eyes swollen, her cheeks creased with the pressure of his suit coat and buttons.

"I knew-" Her words were swallowed in a half sob. Melrose stroked wayward strands of hair behind her ear. She drew a breath. "We always knew it could happen. He was far more ill than he let on, and he pushed himself so hard—"

More tears spilled down her cheeks. Melrose brushed them away with his thumb. "I know."

"Why doesn't that make it easier?"

"It never does." He sighed. "We can only hope in what comes next."

She nodded, sniffling back more tears in an effort to speak. "The House will remain."

"Yes." Bereft of its founder, Regeleus House had fallen into the hands of the Blood Kind council Melrose ruled. The houses of mercy would be well-funded and overseen until Zuri made a decision about who would rule next. As the only heir to Vectorix House, even though absent, she could not carry the burden of another leadership post. "Aleron has agreed to take it under interim management."

"It will be good for him to have other pursuits." A faint smile ghosted her face. "He needs to be distracted."

"Indeed. What will you do, my Zurina?"

Her gaze faltered for a moment, glancing over his shoulder. Her jaw set. Dread filled Melrose. The last time she'd worn that expression, he hadn't heard from her in months, until she had surfaced with the Talamars.

When she met his eyes, her face had hardened further. "I am Vectorix. I will bring Conan to justice. He will harm no one else."

EPILOGUE
HEAD LOCK

Jean-Claude had two kinds of smiles.

The smile that indicated you were amusing, and the smile that indicated you deserved to die in the most creative way possible.

Conan had never received the second smile until that morning, when he reported on Quebec City at one of Jean-Claude's many penthouses. There was little point in hiding it. After the harpy's damnable show with the winds, his master would already know his plans had failed.

"Fascinating. I thought after her delightfully disastrous attempt with that pathetic Talamar magician, Thoth's prized brat had been thoroughly cowed. Apparently, not." Jean-Claude spun his wineglass in the air, pondering its depths. His hands still held his tablet computer.

Conan braced himself lest the glass be flung in his direction. One downside to steering clear of the vampire leader's magic in favor of straightforward brutality. The slim man could kill him without a single physical action.

Conan finally dared to speak. "Such actions are outside of any of our control."

"True. Although at least the other one, the Talamar, is still hiding in his skyscraper. That should do for a while longer." Jean-Claude's smile widened.

Conan nodded. "Very good, Sir."

"Still, you have disappointed me greatly. It seems your own thoughts are turning towards mutiny, perhaps?" The wineglass cracked along the sides, spilling fresh blood mixed with Merlot onto the fine carpet.

"Sir?"

Jean-Claude strolled over to the table that ran the length of the elegant dining room. Round objects lay in a row beneath a black cloth. He placed his tablet next to them. "Tell me, do you enjoy my new decoration?"

He whipped the cloth off, revealing five severed heads. Conan fought to keep his expression neutral, even while his palms sweated.

Harmen. Puchinsky. Tok. Bouvier. Mason.

"Such a waste. Though I hope it has taught you a lesson."

"Yes." Find a more secure inner circle next time. "Will that be all?"

Jean-Claude raised his hand. "One final matter. After this strenuous latest endeavor, I'm certain you could use some time to relax. Therefore, I am reassigning you to Halecraig Castle, on the border of Romania and Hungary. Fine scenery during the summer, and I'm certain you will find the isolation most restful. While it is outfitted with proper communication devices, in order for you to find the maximum amount of peace, your usage of them will be strictly limited and monitored."

Rage flooded Conan's veins and flamed his cheeks. But he knew better than to act on it. "...generous, Sir."

"I thought so. You are dismissed. Your plane departs tomorrow morning from my private airfield. If you are late or absent, well, I suppose my mantelpiece could use a new head."

Jean-Claude flashed another smile.

Conan pivoted stiffly and left the room. He exited the building in a numb haze, mindful of the three vampires who shadowed his footsteps. Well, they were in for a sodding surprise. All he planned on doing was getting as drunk as possible for ten o'clock in the morning.

He plowed through the stream of tourists that flocked downtown Quebec City. All of them standing around like idiots with their cameras out and their mouths agape, marveling at the old architecture intermingling with the new.

One fool was even attempting to climb a stone archway that spanned the road separating the old city from the rest of the downtown area. A woman with brilliant red hair and sunglasses beckoned to him from the top, looking out from between two crenels.

Such fine hair. But the face ruined the effect, as it was far too clever and mischievous. Still, some time with a woman wouldn't be amiss. Particularly after the failure with Mistress Zurina. There was no sign of her now. Likely, she had nestled herself between the renewed protection of Vir Vectorix and the shelter of Aleron Talamar.

The hag would face her reckoning.

He continued down the street, stepping briskly around street musicians and yet more aimless tourists.

A delicate shoulder bumped into his. "Whoops! Sorry."

"Hm. Yes, you are." Conan glanced down at the girl, a slender thing who clutched a map.

Then he looked again, into sharp gray eyes set in a heart-shaped face with a sprinkling of freckles across her pert nose and sunset red hair falling down her back. His mouth suddenly dried. For a moment, it was winter. The girl wore a velvet and wool coat, and her eyes shone in pure adoration.

Conan's heart leaped. A vision of perfection. Identical in every way.

He'd finally found her doppelganger.

"Karina."

She shook her head, her eyebrow raised. "No, I'm Harper."

That belief have to be altered in short order.

"Forgive me." He swallowed, summoning all of his mesmerizing power. One of the few useful things his Talamar ancestry had granted. "You seem lost. May I help you find your way?"

Her eyes dilated slightly as his charisma worked on her mind. Then she blinked. "Um, I guess? I'm looking for this old hall that has incredible foundation work and structure."

"I know of a place. I'm certain it is so beautiful, you'll never want to leave."

"Really? Sign me up." She grinned and accepted his proffered arm.

Halecraig Castle suddenly seemed a most advantageous getaway.

Acknowledgements

Forever thanks goes to God, the first Creator. Also, a million tons of appreciation to Julia Busko. Here's to perseverance—we did it and we're both still alive! Let's keep this up. Another vat of gratitude to Sarah White, who put up with all of my pointed questions and debating as I worked through her editorial feedback (and she never resorted to the Duct Tape Solution). Thanks to Rachel Kennedy for bothering me literally every single day for new installments. Your Story-Eater skills are legendary. Finally, thanks to Lisa Walker England for pushing me to start Blood Mercy: Thicker Than Water as an online serial. It was scary but a lot of fun!

-Janeen Ippolito

Thanks to my husband for putting up with all the stress I've been under—and helping me through it all. And here's to you, Janeen, and the story that brought us together! To Sarah White, for helping keep Janeen and I sane through this process, and for her hard work editing the book. And to the Creator, for bringing all this together.

- Julia Busko

Aleron Talamar is in trouble, and this time,
not even the priesthood can save him.

BLOOD MERCY
THE DARKEST STAIN

coming soon

After the death of her husband, Zurina Vectorix must take up her birthright to stop the ruthless Conan Talamar. But her search forces her to face the life she left 80 years ago.

Aleron Talamar is doing all he can to help Zuri, the woman who raised him. But when she returns home with runaway Harper McAllister, Aleron must cope with a young woman whose very appearance evokes his own dark secrets.

Learn more at www.bloodmercy.wordpress.com

FROM UNCOMMON UNIVERSES PRESS

 Julia Busko (like "bus" and "co") is an illustrator, designer, writer, and the Elusive Unicorn (art director) of Uncommon Universes Press. She has created book covers for Janeen Ippolito, made logos and t-shirt designs, and is planning a series of steampunk fairy tale picture books. In her spare time she dances with a local company and watches documentaries and horror movies. She strives for art filled with creative wonder and the beauty inherent in tragedy. Go to juliabusko.com to dive into her world of remarkable visions and artistic musings.

Connect With Me Online!

Facebook: www.facebook.com/JuliabuskoIllustrator

Website: www.juliabusko.com

Instagram: juliabuskoillustration

Pinterest: Julia Busko

Janeen Ippolito is an idea-charged teacher, reader, writer, book reviewer, and the Fearless Leader (president) of Uncommon Universes Press. She writes nonfiction writing help and speculative fiction laced with horror, humor, and cultural tension. In her nonexistent spare time she reads, cooks, and sword-fights. Two of her dreams are to eat a fried tarantula and to travel to Antarctica. Go to janeenippolito.com for world-building resources and off-the-wall insights from this sleep-deprived author.

Connect With Me Online!

Facebook: www.facebook.com/janeenippolitowriter

Twitter: @TheQuietPen

Website: www.janeenippolito.com

Instagam: janeen_ippolito

Goodreads: www.goodreads.com/author/show/14112384.Janeen_Ippolito

Pinterest: Janeen Ippolito

49837567R00089

Made in the USA
San Bernardino, CA
06 June 2017